Here I Rogue Again

Rogues of Redemption, Book 5

By
Brenna Ash

© Copyright 2025 by Brenna Ash
Text by Brenna Ash
Cover by Dar Albert

Dragonblade Publishing, Inc. is an imprint of Kathryn Le Veque Novels, Inc.
P.O. Box 23
Moreno Valley, CA 92556
ceo@dragonbladepublishing.com

Produced in the United States of America

First Edition June 2025
Print Edition

Reproduction of any kind except where it pertains to short quotes in relation to advertising or promotion is strictly prohibited.

All Rights Reserved.

The characters and events portrayed in this book are fictitious. Any similarity to real persons, living or dead, is purely coincidental and not intended by the author.

ARE YOU SIGNED UP FOR DRAGONBLADE'S BLOG?

You'll get the latest news and information on exclusive giveaways, exclusive excerpts, coming releases, sales, free books, cover reveals and more.

Check out our complete list of authors, too!

No spam, no junk. That's a promise!

Sign Up Here

www.dragonbladepublishing.com

Dearest Reader;

Thank you for your support of a small press. At Dragonblade Publishing, we strive to bring you the highest quality Historical Romance from some of the best authors in the business. Without your support, there is no 'us', so we sincerely hope you adore these stories and find some new favorite authors along the way.

Happy Reading!

CEO, Dragonblade Publishing

Additional Dragonblade books by Author Brenna Ash

Rogues of Redemption Series
Sweet Rogue O' Mine (Book 1)
Rogue You Like a Hurricane (Book 2)
No Rogue Like You (Book 3)
Nobody's Rogue (Book 4)
Here I Rogue Again (Book 5)

The Lyon's Den Series
The Lyon's Last Gamble

CHAPTER ONE

Kincardine, Scotland
1816

GUNN BURNETT'S EYES scanned the sparse clientele at the Thistle & Pig, and wondered how he could turn things around. He'd owned the pub for years, but it was bleeding money now and had been for months. And he had no idea why.

Ever since he'd returned from the war over a year ago, he'd been less and less profitable until now where he was nearly in the negative on a daily basis, bringing in just a pittance of income compared to before when the pub thrived. He just didn't understand what had caused everyone to turn away.

For the most part, patrons had slowly stopped coming. A person here. A person there. Until soon he was lucky to see a handful of people walk through the door. His connected inn wasn't faring much better.

"Do ye need me to stay?" his barkeep Thomas asked. The man had been tending the bar for him since he'd taken ownership of the Thistle & Pig and Gunn felt a twinge of guilt kenning he would need to cut his employment in the near future.

"Nay. Go home to your wife and enjoy your evening," Gunn offered, trying to keep his demeanor upbeat even though he felt the blanket of defeat beginning to cover him and block out the sun.

Thomas smiled, the gesture showing a crooked front tooth, and his face lit up at the mention of his wife. "She will verra much like to see me home early."

Gunn nodded and gave him a half-hearted smile. "Have a good night, Thomas."

Surely the man had to ken something was amiss. He'd seen how the Thistle & Pig went from thriving where every chair and table would be filled each night to now being barely able to seat a person at the bar.

"Hell," Gunn mumbled, pushing his hand though his short hair, and slapped the towel that he'd just used to wipe down the bar against his leg with enough force he felt the pinch through his breeches.

He hadn't always owned this business, but he'd kenned of it since his younger years, when his father would bring him along on his business deals. Those consisted of how he could figure out a way to divest whoever he was meeting with from his coin. The man would have rather spent his days scheming than doing an honest day's work. Gunn never understood it.

When his father passed, and Gunn became Laird of Leys, at the too young age of 16, he'd made a vow to restore the name of Burnett. It had been a prideful, good name before his father had tarnished it over time with his shady deals and dishonest bartering.

It took years, but Gunn was able to salvage the name and their reputation and soon they were thriving once again. One thing his father taught him was a keen business sense. Only Gunn used that for good. He wasn't out to swindle anyone.

The previous owner of the pub and inn was someone Gunn looked up to. He was the one person that didn't seem to fall for his father's schemes and Gunn admired him for that. When he took ill and was unable to maintain the upkeep required to stay in business, Gunn saw it as a good investment opportunity. Gunn also didn't want to see it fall into disrepair, not when the owner had worked so hard to make it a place where the townsfolk could gather and enjoy a drink and visitors could eat a hearty meal and relax while traveling. He offered to purchase it and the Thistle & Pig had been his ever since.

"Good eve, Burnett," his last remaining customer said with a wave.

Gunn gave him a nod. "Smythe. Have a good e'ening."

Once Smythe exited the door, Gunn looked around his now empty pub and not expecting anyone else to enter, he began wiping down tables and putting up chairs.

As he worked, he focused on his failing business. He needed to do something. A new cook, mayhap? Nay. His cook was one of the best. A redesign of the space? Just the thought gave Gunn a headache. The cost of that would entail more than he could afford.

The door whisked open.

"We're closed," Gunn announced without turning. *Damn it.* He should have locked the door and turned the open sign to closed when he had the chance. He had no desire to prolong this miserable night.

"Oh," a feminine voice responded. "I apologize," she said quietly from the doorway.

Gunn spun at the unfamiliar voice and his eyes widened. A waif of a woman stood there, nervously fidgeting with the dainty pendant hanging from her slim neck. She was much too thin. Much too pale. And were those fading bruises darkening her delicate skin?

Immediately he called out to her. "Wait."

She paused, one hand reaching out to clench the door handle so tightly her knuckles turned white.

"Ye needna leave."

The woman shook her head, causing the wisps of blonde hair peeking out from her gray bonnet to fly in the air. "If you are closed, I can find another place."

English.

The lass was English. It had been some time since an English woman had graced his pub. "What is it that ye need?" He asked, his voice sounding gruffer than he intended.

She rolled her lips inward and shuffled her feet nervously. "I was just looking to get out of the cold for the night. Might you have a room? I promise not to ask aught else of you."

The undertone of desperation in her voice pierced his heart. The melancholy that ebbed from her in waves had him wondering how she'd managed to find herself here. What had happened that she sought out a room in a foreign land from a stranger—alone. He looked behind her and didn't see anyone accompanying her.

He sighed. He couldn't turn her away.

"Of course. I'm closing the pub for the night, but the inn is open." Walking to the door, she quickly stepped out of his way, and he locked it, turning the sign hanging on the door to closed. He gave the woman what he hoped was a welcoming smile.

"Follow me," he ordered.

Making his way through the pub, he entered the connecting door that led into the inn. He held it open until she passed through, then closed it and engaged the lock.

"Do ye have any bags?"

She shook her head and held up a small worn leather bag that had seen better days. "Just this one."

His brows furrowed. He found that just as odd as her being alone.

At the desk that held the booking ledger, Gunn scanned the page. Though he wasn't sure why. Currently, there wasn't anyone renting any of his available rooms.

"Name?"

Her big blue eyes darted to the door, looking worried as if someone might see her or hear her name. Her reaction reminded him of a mouse backed into a corner by a starving cat, searching for any means of escape.

"Are ye well?" he asked.

Turning to him, she gave him a faltering smile. "I'm sorry. Jocelyn."

"Well, Jocelyn, 'tis nice to make your acquaintance," he said cheerily, trying to lighten the mood and set her at ease. "I'm Gunn, the owner, and ye've arrived at a time that all of my rooms happen to be available. Do ye have a preference? Front room. Second floor. Back room."

"Second floor, back room, please."

She was frightened of something. Or someone. That was evident from the way her eyes kept darting around the lobby of the inn and the way she hadn't stopped wringing her hands since they'd entered.

"Of course. 'Twill be five shillings, please."

Her eyes rounded and she took a deep breath as she opened her reticule and pulled out a small coin bag.

The lack of jingles from coins rubbing against each other led Gunn to believe that the woman didn't have a lot of money. Shite. She wouldn't be the salvation he was looking for. Not one to take a person's last coin, he cleared his throat.

"My apologies. Ye said ye wanted a back room, aye?"

"I do, if you have one available."

He chuckled. "I most definitely do. But I stated the wrong price. My back rooms are one shilling."

Her brows drew together in confusion. "Surely, you jest. They must cost more than that."

They did, but he wasn't about to admit that to her. The lass looked like she had been through enough rough times and he didn't want to add to her burdens, whatever they may be.

"Nay, I wouldna do such a thing. One shilling."

Her slim shoulders dropped in visible relief. In the light of the inn, he could see that the shading on her face was certainly fading bruises.

Instantly his fists clenched. His protective instinct kicked in. He inhaled a deep breath, trying to calm his irritation. He didn't want to frighten her more than she already was. Men that laid their hands on women in a violent manner were naught but cowards. So unsure of themselves that they needed to beat women into submission so that they felt strong. Gunn held back a scoff. Bastards like that were aught but weaklings that needed to be shown how their fists and kicks felt on their own body.

He'd gladly teach the lesson.

Handing him the shilling, she noticed the way he watched her and tugged on her bonnet, bringing it down to cover more of her face. Trying to hide the marks no doubt.

It didn't work. There were too many.

And then the whole situation hit him. Where had she come from? Was she traveling alone? That was dangerous. Where was her chaperone? Her parents? She looked old enough to not need to be in the company of her parents, but still, she shouldn't be traveling alone. Mayhap her parents were the cause of her bruises. That just angered him further.

"Are ye alone?" He had no right asking her that. The poor lass looked wary enough already. He didn't need to add to that.

The blues of her eyes darkened, as her brows drew down. "Why do you ask? I do not think that is any business of yours, sir." She said defensively, tilting her chin up in a sign of strength.

He admired her tenacity.

Gunn held his hands up. "I mean no offense. I just dinna come across many young women traveling alone."

She straightened her shoulders. "I am more than capable of taking care of myself," she said curtly.

In that moment, with the amount of conviction lacing her voice, she almost had him convinced. But not quite. Sensing that there was more to her story than the few things she'd said, he let it go. Although she was putting on a brave front, she seemed frightened. Wary of something.

Or mayhap someone.

Either way, he wanted her to feel that she was safe here, so he grabbed the key off the wall and motioned for her to follow him. He'd just met the lass. Pushing her for information would only scare her away. Something he didn't want to do. The poor woman looked like she could really use a place to rest. If naught else, he wanted to be able to offer that small comfort to her.

As they ascended the stairs, he tried to make small conversation, but she didn't engage.

He'd chosen the last room on the left for her. Unlocking the door, he pushed it open. "Here ye go."

With one last glance over her shoulder, she entered the room and dropped her travel bag onto the bed. "May I have the key?"

"Of course," he remained in the hall, but reached out to drop the key in her waiting palm. "If ye are hungry, I can have a plate brought up to ye. I dinna ken how far ye have traveled, but, and again, I mean no offense, but ye look like ye could use a good meal."

Worrying her bottom lip with her teeth, she shook her head. "Thank you. I am fine, though."

He got the feeling she was aught but fine. "I will have Cook put something together and have it brought up. 'Tis on the house."

She put her hands up. "No, I can't let you do that."

He admired her want to pay for everything. But she looked like she needed a respite, and he was happy to be the one to offer it. "'Tis included in the cost of the room. All meals are," he quickly added. "So, in the morn, make sure to come down to break your fast. Cook is one of the best in town. Ye dinna want to miss her scones."

Nodding, she ran her palms down her sides. "I thank you again. You are being much too kind."

"If ye need aught else, please let me ken. I shall take care of it straightaway. Good night." He closed the door and not a second later he heard the key being inserted and the lock engaging.

She was a bonnie lass, but there was a reason she was here. Her nerves were on high alert, both when she arrived and when she got to the room. He hoped that it wasn't him that worried her.

Granted, he was a large man. A boxer. A fighter. He'd held the position of bouncer at many an establishment, including his own. But he would never hurt her, or any other woman.

She had him intrigued. There was mystery behind her eyes, and he wanted to unravel it.

JOCELYN TOWNSEND DIDN'T breathe a sigh of relief until she turned the key in the lock, solidifying her safety from anyone on the other side of the door.

The innkeeper seemed pleasant enough, handsome even, though his hulking stature gave her pause. He looked like he could snap her in half if he wanted to. She didn't feel unsafe around him. Just the opposite actually.

For the first time in a long time, she felt safe.

The way the innkeeper carried himself—straight-shouldered, sure of himself—it reminded her of men she'd seen in the past that had served in the military. Mayhap he had as well.

Moving to the one window in the room, she checked the latch.

Locked.

Good. Second floor or not, the window would remain locked at all times. Same with the door.

She was sure the innkeeper—she knew he had given her his name, but her mind was so busy, she couldn't remember it—was suspicious of her. He had noticed straightaway that she didn't have a chaperone accompanying her. She shouldn't be surprised.

When she'd left her home in the middle of the night in Rochester, the last thing she had thought about was what it would look like to someone. She was just happy to be out of the house.

Away from *him*.

Away from his hurtful words.

Away from his brutal punches.

Spreading her palms on her stomach, the surge of protection washing over her was almost overwhelming as she thought of the life growing within her. She sighed.

It was why she finally left. She could take her husband's mistreatment. But the babe? No. She wouldn't stand by while he beat her and harmed the baby. The babe was innocent. It didn't deserve the same hate Victor showed to her. Once she'd found out she was pregnant, she had made up her mind to leave.

It was something she had been thinking about a lot in recent months, but the babe had forced her to move everything into motion. The minute she thought she may be with child, she began planning. She had already been hiding away a shilling here. A shilling there. It was enough so she could run, but she didn't have much left.

The journey here took most of her savings. Tomorrow she would approach the innkeeper and ask for employment.

Surely, he could use help. She had many skills. Cleaning, cooking, she even knew how to bookkeep. If he needed help in any of those areas, she could offer her services. Then she could secure permanent lodgings. Hopefully, she traveled far enough that Victor wouldn't find her here.

Her belief was that he wouldn't suspect that she would head north to Scotland. Her family was from southern England. Well, they were. They had passed on. But south was where all her friends were. Not that she could call them friends now. They surely weren't. She hadn't spoken to them since her marriage to Victor.

He had always said she was being selfish to give them attention that she should be giving to him. He was a very jealous man. After a few times of trying to reach out to her friends, and then bearing his wrath, she decided it was easier to let them go. Though it saddened her to do so.

Things were much calmer when she stayed home as he demanded and did what he ordered. At first, she thought it was just the way marriages went, even though she'd never seen her parents act in such a way, but they were older.

She knew better. She was much too smart for that. Plenty of married people around her were perfectly happy in their union. And the women that she knew were not beat by their husbands. Only Victor did that. Jocelyn realized early on that no matter how *well-behaved* she was, the beatings would still continue.

She saw everyone else in their happy marriages and longed for the same thing for herself.

Now that she was no longer under Victor's heavy hand, it was as if a weight had been lifted off her shoulders. She could breathe.

She was free.

Jocelyn sat on the bed and bounced up and down a couple of times on the soft mattress. This was one of the finer inns she'd stayed in on her travels. The bed was even nicer than the one she slept in at home.

Home.

She needed to stop referring to Rochester as home. It had never felt that way to her and she was happy to be gone from there.

A yawn overtook her. She was tired. So tired.

She could collapse right here and sleep for days.

A knock sounded, and she straightened, her nerves suddenly on edge.

"Miss Jocelyn. My laird asked me to put a plate together for ye. Said ye looked like ye could use a hearty meal."

Approaching the door slowly, she put her ear against it. Listening for noises in the hall. Something that would alert her to the servant not being alone. But she heard naught.

"Miss?"

Thinking she was being overcautious, she sighed. The chances of Victor finding her here were low. She needed to stop thinking he would. Turning the key, she opened the door. A girl who looked no more than ten and six stood there with a full tray in her arms, a warm, welcoming smile on her face. "If ye dinna mind, I will set this on the table?"

Looking around the girl, Jocelyn noted that the hall was empty. She rolled her eyes. She really needed to stop thinking that Victor would appear around every corner.

"Of course, please come in."

The scent of roast venison curled around her. Loudly, her stomach let out a growl.

The servant girl smiled. "Ye will enjoy this meal that Cook prepared. She's the best in town." She set the tray down and moved the covered plate onto the table. "I also brought some tea. I thought ye might like some with your meal."

"Thank you. You're very kind."

The girl dipped down into a curtsy. "I'm Flora. If ye need aught, please ask. I will be more than happy to bring it to ye."

"This should be more than enough, Flora. Please tell your laird I am very thankful."

With a smile, the girl exited, and Jocelyn rushed over to lock the door once again.

Laird. Did that mean he led a clan or something similar? Or was it the equivalent of Lord in England so he was a landowner? She wasn't familiar with titles in Scotland.

As much as she wanted to stand there and ponder about the laird, the smells coming from the covered plate beckoned her, consuming her attention.

She lifted the cover, and her eyes widened at the delicious spread on the plate. Venison, crusty bread, roasted vegetables. The smells that filled the room were heavenly.

With an appetite that acted like she hadn't eaten in days, Jocelyn ripped into the bread, dipping it into the sauce covering the venison. As soon as it hit her tongue, she moaned. Delicious was an understatement. Before she knew it, she'd cleared the plate and drunk two cups of tea. Underneath a smaller covered plate, she found a lemon curd tart. Savoring the delectable treat, she ate it in small bites, wanting it to last.

They weren't lying when they said their cook was the best in town. Jocelyn believed she should be regaled to points farther. With such talent, she didn't dare offer her cooking skills. She couldn't hold a candle to the food she'd just eaten.

Her stomach full, she unpacked the few items in her travel bag. Most everything she owned was left behind at the house she'd shared with Victor. There just wasn't enough space for her to carry more. She only took a couple gowns and some undergarments. All her gowns looked the same. Victor insisted that she only wore gray. It was drab and the color washed out her skin, making her look even more pale than she was.

But he didn't care.

Her hand closed around the small leather-bound diary. It had belonged to her mother and was the only item she had to remind her of her parents. They'd passed a few years ago, and Victor had sold off their house, including everything inside.

She'd managed to sneak the diary out from her mother's possessions without him knowing and had kept it hidden ever since. When she'd left, she'd made sure to grab it.

The entries were from when her mother was young. She loved to read through her mama's thoughts about society. Her friends. Her family. When she met papa. The diary had offered Jocelyn comfort when things got too much to bear.

As she settled into bed, she read a few entries, her mother's delicate handwriting bringing a smile to her face. Tucking the diary under her pillow when she was done, she snuffed the candle and snuggled into the thick duvet.

Within seconds, exhaustion took over and she was drifting off to a peaceful sleep.

CHAPTER TWO

GUNN HAD BEEN on edge all morning as he waited for Jocelyn to come down to the dining room to break her fast. Flora had informed him that she was very grateful for the meal last night.

He scoffed. A simple meal wasn't anything to be so thankful for. The poor lass looked like she hadn't eaten a hearty meal in a long time. She could use to put on some weight. She looked far too frail.

Or mayhap it was the dim light.

Seeing her in the sunlight would show him if his original assessment was correct.

Flora hurried into the room.

"My laird. Miss Jocelyn is on her way down," she whispered excitedly, then threw her shoulders back when Jocelyn walked into the dining room. "Miss Jocelyn, I have readied this table for ye." Pointing to a table, Flora waited for Jocelyn to sit before grabbing the tea pot.

Gunn noticed the way her eyes scanned the room before her shoulders relaxed. It was almost as if she was looking for someone. She folded her napkin on her lap and thanked Flora for the tea she poured.

There were so many questions he wanted to ask. But they all felt intrusive. Instead, he went with pleasantries and small talk once Flora left for the kitchen.

"Good morn. I hope ye have enjoyed your stay?"

She took a sip of tea, her tongue darting out to catch a drop on her lip and nodded.

His eyes tracked her tongue and he tugged at his collar. The room suddenly felt a wee bit warm.

"I did. You have been most kind, and the meal last night was delicious. You must give my compliments to your cook."

"She will be glad to hear that. Flora will be out shortly with scones, jam, and clotted cream. Please let her ken if ye require aught else."

He left the room for fear that he would ply her with questions. Not one to usually be the curious type, that was an area his friend, Malcolm, dominated. That man was curious about everything.

But for some reason, he just couldn't get the questions about the woman to stop swirling about his head.

In his study, he sank into his chair and opened his books. Dread overcame him at the numbers listed there. Most of them in the negative. The last thing he could afford to do was rent out a room at a fifth of the cost. His conscience wouldn't let him take advantage though. It wasn't in his blood.

He wasn't his father.

Nay, something in the reserved way Jocelyn spoke and acted let him ken that there was something amiss with her. He'd just met the lass, and yet an overwhelming sense of protectiveness washed over him. He didn't get it. He'd never had this reaction to a lass before, especially one he'd just met.

He refocused on the numbers in the ledger spread out in front of him. If something didn't change soon, he would either have to close the Thistle & Pig or sell it.

Neither of those were options he wanted to consider.

Failure had him slumping his shoulders. He just didn't understand. Before he'd left to fight, it had been a thriving establishment. When he'd returned, it was barely staying afloat, and the money he'd set aside from its earnings had dwindled away.

His head snapped up at the knock on his door.

"Theodore," he greeted, standing up and extending his hand for a shake.

"Gunn. Ye look like ye havena slept for days. What ails ye?"

He pushed his hands through his short hair. "I just wish I had an explanation for how e'erything went wrong."

With a frown, the man looked around the room.

Theodore MacInnis had managed the establishment for Gunn while he was away. He'd kenned him for years and had full confidence in his ability to take care of the business while he was away.

Coming home to it on the verge of closing was not what he was expecting.

He sighed. "Looking o'er the books is misery."

"I see ye've got a new customer. Bonny lass, she is," he chirped, changing the subject.

"Aye, though, I am no' charging her full price. And I'm giving her the meals for free, so she'll hardly be my salvation."

Theodore clucked his tongue. "Following those business practices, 'tis no wonder ye arena making any profit."

"Ye arena funny. The lass looked like she needed a helping hand. I couldna say nay."

Theodore wagged his finger at him in the air. "See. That is where ye are losing money. Ye are too soft."

Gunn barked out a laugh. "Now that is comical. At no point in my life has anyone e'er accused me of being too soft." Anything but, actually. He had a reputation around town for being one not to mess with. Well known in the boxing clubs, he still remained undefeated. Proud of it, too. And when things got too rowdy in the pub, it was he who single-handedly removed the rabble-rousers.

"Who is she?" Theodore asked, interest lighting his brown eyes.

For some reason, his interest in Jocelyn irked Gunn.

"Just a lass passing through. I dinna ken how long she will be staying."

It wasn't a lie.

"Well, if ye arena charging her, chances are strong she'll stay for quite some time."

Gunn narrowed his eyes. "I dinna think she is here to take advantage of me, if that is what ye are suggesting." He walked over to the sideboard and poured two glasses of whisky and handed one to Theodore. Savoring the burn as the amber liquid smoothed its way down his throat, he wet his lips. "She appears to have had a rough time of it. I only want to make her journey a little easier."

Theodore harrumphed, his expression letting Gunn ken that he didn't believe him. "How long have ye been saying that to yourself to get ye to believe it?" He chuckled, sipping his whisky.

"Enough about my guests. Is there something that ye need? Ye arena due to work this week."

As the manager, Gunn had kept Theodore on, but he'd severely cut back on the time he spent here. This was a week he'd given him off.

Theodore shrugged, and picked at a piece of lint on his trousers. "I just wanted check in to see how ye fare."

"Ye ken how the business is struggling. If ye have any idea on how to make the patrons come back, I'd appreciate it."

"'Tis such a shame." Theodore shook his head, his lips pursed. "The Thistle & Pig used to be such a thriving business. It seems e'eryone has moved on to other pubs."

"My whisky is just as good, if no' better, than anyone else's. I've got the finest cook. The cleanest rooms. I need to think of something or I'm going to have to close its doors."

With raised brows, Theodore assessed him. "'Tis that bad? Are ye certain?"

"'Tis bad. Verra bad. I already have ye working half your time. I've let some people go. My mind is open to suggestions, but whate'er they are, they need to be quick because I feel like I'm on a sinking ship when it comes to this place."

"Thankfully, ye've got your other businesses and properties. Surely ye could move around money if needed."

"Aye, mayhap I could. But I dinna want to throw it away, which is what I feel like I would be doing if I just keep pushing money in this place."

It was a lie. He had already put the spare money he had into the pub. Truth be told, there wasn't anything left for him to give. His estates were running on the bare minimum. Luckily, he'd been able to retain his staff there, but if he took any more losses, that wouldn't be the case for much longer. He was desperate.

Desperate.

The word tasted sour on his tongue.

But his problems were his own. He wasn't about to announce to the world just how dire his situation had grown to be. The Thistle & Pig needed to thrive once again. When it did, everything would right itself.

Gunn just needed to figure out how to turn it around.

Theodore stood. "Well, I am sure ye will think of something. I must go. I've got business elsewhere, but I wanted to check in. I shall see ye next week."

Gunn watched him leave and sank back into his chair, cradling his head in his hands as he stared at the ceiling. What could he do?

Failure was not an option. He wouldn't be able to face his friends with a failed business. They had already warned him of the purchase years ago, but he wouldn't listen. He needed this to be successful just to prove them wrong.

JOCELYN WAITED FOR the laird to re-enter the dining hall, but after Flora returned three times asking her if she needed anything else, she came to the conclusion that he was off on business.

She had wanted to approach him about employment. "Flora. Do

you know when the laird will return?"

"I dinna ken, miss. Shall I give him a message when he does?"

Jocelyn thought for a moment and then shook her head. "No, thank you. I will try to catch him later. Thank you for breakfast. Your laird was right when he said your cook made the best scones. They were divine."

Leaving the dining hall, she made her way up to her room. Mayhap she should have a look around town and see what other establishments were there. Maybe one was advertising for help.

Securing her reticule around her wrist, she exited her room, locking the door behind her. Downstairs, there was still no sign of the laird, so she left the inn to familiarize herself with the town.

The inn was near the town center, which Jocelyn found quite quaint. The vernacular buildings added charm and made the street seem welcoming. The cobblestoned streets were clean and there was a crispness in the air that reminded her of autumn and warm apple cider. A treat her mother would always purchase this time of year. Jocelyn would always savor that first sip as she sat on the bench in their small garden, watching the turning leaves sway in the wind, their vibrant colors splashed against the gray sky.

Or perhaps she was reading into it because that's what she wanted it to be. At this point, she had no choice but to make a home here. She was at the end of her coin. Thankfully, it ran out in a town that looked like it could be one she could settle in.

Blend in.

That's all she really wanted. To meld in with society and not be bothered.

As she walked along, she passed a printing press, a bakery, a modiste.

She paused in front of the modiste's window, peering through the glass. Women lingered inside, chatting with each other as they carefully and excitedly chose the fabric for their new gowns.

How she longed for that. The brilliant colors, the fashionable styles. They would complement her so much more than the drab gray gowns she wore.

She looked down at the dark gray day dress she wore. The color alone made her sad. Never again would she wear this awful, drab color. Peering again through the window of the shop, her eyes flitted over the bright colors, taking note of the ones she liked best.

Once she made some money and got herself settled, she would visit the modiste herself and order a gown.

But it wasn't only pretty gowns she missed and yearned for. She longed for the camaraderie of good friends. Confidants she could share secrets with. Talk over tea, whether the talk be serious or lighthearted. It would be so nice. She missed having a friend's support. She'd been so isolated these last few years with Victor.

Dragging her eyes away from the window, she continued on, pulling her bonnet tighter upon her head as a cool drizzle began to fall.

Drats. The rest of her tour would have to wait. She hurried back to the inn, and by the time she burst through the doors, her bonnet and gown were soaked through.

"Miss Jocelyn!" Flora exclaimed, rushing forward.

"I am fine, Flora. It is just a bit of rain." She held her arms out as water dripped off her sleeves to puddle on the floor.

Flora lifted a brow, unconvinced. "Ye are soaked to the bone. Ye must be freezing."

"It's not that bad. Truly, I am well. There's no need for you to make such a fuss out of something so small." A forceful shiver ripped through her and her teeth began to rattle.

The girl shook her head and tsked. "Ye could catch your death. Let me have a hot bath brought up to ye," she said, not waiting for Jocelyn's agreement. "It will warm ye up and I can launder your gown."

"I-I," Jocelyn stuttered, at a loss for words. Such kindness from strangers was a welcome change.

"Go on," she shooed Jocelyn toward the stairs. "I insist."

"What are ye insisting on now, Flora?" The laird asked as he walked into the reception area, before he noticed Jocelyn and his eyes widened. "What happened to ye, lass?"

"She was walking out in the rain, my laird. Soaked to the bone, she is. I was insisting on a hot bath to warm her up."

He cocked his head, eyeing her up and down, before nodding. "I agree. Ye dinna want to catch an ague from the chill."

"Thank you." Not knowing what else to say, feeling outnumbered and embarrassed from the attention, she quickly dropped into a curtsy. Is that what you do for lairds? She didn't know the proper protocols and didn't want to seem uncultured, so she made the move just in case before leaving the room.

He smiled warmly and Jocelyn noted how the gesture transformed his face. He really was a handsome man. His strong jaw looked like it was carved from stone. A small crook in his nose led her to believe that he may have broken it in the past.

"I shall have Flora bring up tea as well to help get ye warm."

Jocelyn averted her eyes. She shouldn't be staring. "T-t-thank you," Jocelyn called over her shoulder as she ascended the stairs to her room. Moments later, Flora arrived with another servant and together they filled a tub with hot water.

Once the water was so high, Jocelyn was sure it would slosh over the sides the instant she stepped into it, Flora handed her towels and a bar of herbal soap.

"After ye've bathed, just leave your gown outside your door. I will pick it up and bring it to the laundress."

Left alone, she stripped off the soaked garment. Her skin was damp and pimpled in the cool air. Testing the water with her hand, the temperature was perfect. She stepped in and sank into the hot water with a sigh. Instantly the tension melted from her muscles and she relaxed against the back of the tub.

Ever since she'd left Victor, her body had been tense. Her muscles bunched up, ready to flee if she happened to see him on any of her stops.

It was silly, but she felt safe here. She laughed, the sound loud in the empty room. She had only met two people here. Why was she already feeling a sense of peace? It made no sense.

Finishing up her bath, she toweled herself dry and dressed. Running a brush through her hair, she secured it in a chignon at the base of her neck, and gathered her wet gown, rolling it into a ball.

Not wanting to be waited on hand and foot, she refused to leave it outside her door. Since she needed to speak with the laird anyway, she would go downstairs and deliver it to Flora herself.

She found Flora wiping down tables in the dining hall.

"Och, miss. Ye could have left that for me to pick up," she said as she reached for the wet gown.

Jocelyn handed it over. "Do you know where the laird is, by chance? I wish to speak with him if he has a moment."

"I believe he may be in his study." She draped Jocelyn's gown over her arm. "If ye follow me, I'll take ye there."

Jocelyn nodded. "I would appreciate that." She followed Flora through the inn and down a back hallway.

They paused at a heavy wooden door and Flora knocked.

"Aye?" Was the response from the other side.

"My laird, Miss Jocelyn would like to speak to ye."

A few long moments passed, and Jocelyn wondered if he was going to come to the door, before it finally swung open. The smell of cherry tobacco wrapped around her.

His brows raised in surprise. "Is e'rything alright?"

She straightened her shoulders, trying to convey confidence that she didn't necessarily feel. "It is. I wondered if we might have a conversation. If you have time, of course."

"Aye, come in. Please." He stepped aside and swept his arm in front of him, welcoming her inside.

Flora excused herself and scurried down the hall.

"Have a seat," the laird offered, dipping his head toward the front of his desk, where chairs were set up side by side.

Jocelyn sank into the overstuffed wingback chair. The size of it seemed to swallow her up, making her feel small. But it was comfortable.

The laird's study was warm and welcoming. A fire blazed in the hearth. The logs crackled as they burnt, sparks flying up toward the shue. The walls were papered in a dark blue and brown striped pattern. His massive desk was covered with papers, books, and ledgers. He sat in a brown leather chair, his fingers steepled under his chin, watching her with curious eyes.

Straightening, she said, "Thank you for meeting with me. I am sure you are busy, so I appreciate your time." She smoothed the skirt of her gown with her palms, a feeble attempt to calm her nerves. "First, I must apologize. I know you told me your name last night, but I fear that with everything happening, I have forgotten it. I mean no disrespect."

He smiled, showing off straight white teeth. "None taken. Gunn Burnett."

Gunn. Such a unique name. How could she have forgotten that?

"And you are a laird?"

"Aye. Laird of Leys."

"I must apologize once again for not knowing the protocol surrounding Scottish titles."

"Dinna fash. We arena such sticklers for following the rules as ye are in England." He winked.

The gesture caught her off guard, and she momentarily lost her train of thought.

"Do I call ye laird? Or Sir Burnett? Or…"

He chuckled. "Really, ye can call me whate'er suits ye. Gunn is fine, though."

Hanging on the wall behind him was a portrait of him in full military dress.

Pointing to the picture, she met his eyes.

"You served in the military?"

He looked over his shoulder at the portrait and nodded. "Aye." His eyes darkened at the admission. "I served my time in Spain fighting and serving my duty to the Crown."

"That must have been difficult," she said quietly.

He nodded stiffly. "'Twas. I've been back for over a year now. Gladly so."

"Thank you for your service. You are very brave."

He dipped his head in thanks, but said naught further on the subject.

She couldn't imagine the things he'd seen. Jocelyn had heard stories and they were quite disconcerting.

She nodded. "Right. Well, I am certain you are wondering why I'm here."

"Indeed." He looked around his study. "Ye ken 'tis no' proper for us to be here alone. Ye without a chaperone. People may talk."

She pursed her lips. "I am no maiden, sir," she clipped. "I do not need a chaperone."

Gunn raised his hands, palms turned out in defense. "Easy, lass. I dinna ken of your circumstances or how ye came to be in Kincardine. I've a sense ye have your reasons, and ye are free to them. 'Tis just uncommon for a lass to be traveling alone. And dangerous," he added.

"I fared well, as you can see."

He narrowed his eyes. "Did ye? I canna help but notice the fading bruises on your skin. Did ye run into trouble on your travels?"

Jocelyn sucked in a breath. She knew the question would be coming sooner or later. With that expectation, she had concocted a story.

She was hesitant to talk about Victor—and her escape. Who knew if Gunn would turn around and contact her husband and tell him to come collect his wife.

That couldn't happen.

She brought her hand up to rub the corner of her eye. "I fear I am very clumsy. I've never met a door that I haven't run into at least once." She pointed to her face. "Running through an unfamiliar space is not suggested," she said with a self-deprecating smile, hoping she was being convincing.

He did not look convinced though.

CHAPTER THREE

JOCELYN WAS LYING.

If those bruises were the result of running into a door, then Gunn was king. He was a boxer. He kenned what bruises caused by angry fists looked like.

For her to get those bruises as bad as they were, she would have had to run into the door repeatedly. There wasn't just one bruise. There were multiple. Almost healed, so some time had passed since the initial beating.

And a beating is exactly what had happened. He'd bet his title on it.

But it appeared the lass didn't want to tell him of the specifics, so he'd let it go.

For now.

"Well, it appears that door held some anger toward ye." He smiled, trying to lighten the mood.

Her soft laugh filled his study, cutting through the tension.

"What is it ye wanted to speak to me about?" he asked, figuring it was better to steer conversation away from what she was uncomfortable speaking about.

"Ah, yes." She straightened in the chair, her tone growing serious. "I would like to settle in Kincardine and wanted to inquire if you had any open positions."

Gunn blew out an exasperated breath, pushing his hand through his hair. Out of all the questions that he thought would pop out of her mouth, that wasn't one of them. It was apparent that she needed money, but he was on the verge of losing his inn and pub. He'd already let staff go. He certainly didn't have the resources to hire someone new.

The pleading in her eyes nearly broke him.

"Why Kincardine?"

"Pardon?" She seemed surprised at his question.

"Kincardine. Why here? 'Tis no' like we are a common stop on the way to other cities. We're just a small town."

Jocelyn worried her bottom lip so hard that Gunn was sure it would bleed at any moment.

He also found himself thinking how much he wanted nibble on it.

"It's a lovely town," she finally said, but offered naught further.

"'Tis," he agreed, nodding. There was no doubt about that. Just inland a ways from the east coast, the sea was close enough that if the wind blew just right, one could smell the brine in the air. "But ye still didna answer my question, lass."

Her eyes darted around the room, though what she was searching for, he hadn't any clue. "I didn't have aught to keep me in England any longer. I've always heard about the rugged beauty of Scotland, and I decided to see for myself." She sighed, jutting her chin out. "The rumors were true, by the way," she added, leaning toward him with a smile.

She was trying to win him over.

It might be working.

"What skills do ye have?" The question was out of his mouth before he could stop it. He closed his eyes, pressing his lips into a thin line. Christ. What was he doing?

Her whole demeanor brightened at his question.

"Well, until I tasted your cook's divine meals, I thought I could cook fairly well." She chuckled. "So, I will not be offering my cooking skills to you. However, I can clean, though you have Flora, and she appears to be more than capable. Maybe I can assist her. But I can also bookkeep."

He raised an eyebrow at that last part. "You bookkeep? As in accounts? Ledgers?"

She nodded. "Yes. It's a skill taught to me by father."

"Your father?"

"Yes. Lord Bixby. Oh." She clamped her hand over her mouth, and he got the feeling she had said more than she intended.

Feigning disinterest in the name, he made a mental note to investigate the name later. "'Tis uncommon for fathers to teach their daughters bookkeeping."

"True, but he wanted me to be self-aware when it came to my future assets." She let out a cynical laugh. "I will say that neither of us had foreseen my current plight. As you can tell, I have no assets to keep books over. But I am very knowledgeable when it comes to such things."

Gunn thought about the current state of his books. The money he was losing as if he was running it through a sieve. Mayhap, he could have her review the ledgers from when he was away and identify where things started to go wrong.

"I canna offer ye much. A pound a month, a room, and your meals."

Her eyes widened. "That is more than generous."

"We have a deal?"

She jumped up from her chair, clasping her hands in front of her chest. "Yes, yes. Thank you."

"Dinna thank me yet. I've a specific job for ye that may have ye running for the door."

She shook her head. "I doubt that. When shall I start?"

He appreciated her eagerness, but he needed time to gather the ledgers.

"On the morrow?"

"Yes. That is perfect. Where shall I report?"

"Here, after ye break your fast."

"I will be here." She moved to leave, but he stopped her for one last question.

"Jocelyn?"

She spun and looked at him. "Yes?"

"Is your last name also Bixby?"

She shook her head. "It's Townsend." With that she rushed from the room.

He blew out a breath, and sat staring at the ceiling, his hands cradling his head. What in the hell was he doing? Straightening, he reached into his desk drawer and withdrew a piece of parchment, ink, and a quill. He penned a letter to his friend, sharing his concerns, and asking him to look into the matter.

She didn't share the same name as her father. There could be many different reasons why. He may not be her real father. Which in that case, it was very kind of him to take on Jocelyn as his own. Or she could be married. Widowed.

Malcolm could find out those things easily, he was certain. He had served under Wellington and done reconnaissance work for the effort. He'd even uncovered a traitor that had been selling secrets to the enemy.

Gunn remembered they were actually due to meet in a few days. Pinching the bridge of his nose, he tried to clear his head. How had he forgotten that? He would ask his good friend for his assistance in the matter when they met.

If her father was indeed a lord, why would she come to Scotland? Was he cruel? And how did she not have any money?

More so, why would she want to work? Gunn could easily name off a handful of young women that he kenned and were daughters of titled men. Work was the last thing on their minds. They were too busy trying to find a suitable husband.

Certainly, Malcolm would find out.

So many questions swirled around his head about the circumstances of her mysterious appearance.

'I am no maiden, sir.'

Her words kept playing over and over in his head. Had she been compromised in some way? He didn't believe so. She wasn't broken. She had a strong spirit. Defeated? Aye, that was a better descriptor when it came to the bonny woman.

Ugh, he pushed his hands through his short hair. He would drive himself daft thinking about all the possibilities.

He slipped the letter that he'd written into the top drawer of his desk. He would see Malcolm faster than they could exchange correspondence, so there was no need to make sure Flora got it to a carrier.

With that settled, he started the arduous task of digging out all the ledgers he wanted Jocelyn to review. There were several. As they started to pile up on his desk, he felt bad for what he was going to task Jocelyn with.

If she was as proficient as she said, then mayhap she could make heads or tails out of the mess his business was. It was a task that he should have tackled on his own, but with trying to keep everything afloat, he just hadn't had the time.

Pouring himself a whisky, he took a long pull, emptying the glass. He swallowed with a hiss and refilled his glass.

It had been some time since all of his friends had gotten together. Now that they were all married and most of them either with wee ones or bairns on the way, it was harder for all of them to gather. This situation had him missing them.

Mayhap he should send word and invite them all down to Leyson Castle. They could bring their wives and children.

Mind made up, he retrieved his inkwell and parchment. Thirty minutes later, he had his invitations ready to send. He'd hand them to Flora to send out when he saw her later.

JOCELYN STARED AT the stacks of ledgers piled high on the desk in front of her. Gunn had tasked her to review them to see if she could identify issues that might explain some financial issues the inn and pub had been having. He hadn't explained much more than that and she didn't question him on it.

"Well," she said into the empty room. "I might as well get into it."

Gunn had kindly set up a workspace for her in a room that looked like it was used for storage. Trunks and crates were stacked against one wall, but she couldn't tell what they held. Some were nailed shut and others held items wrapped in canvas.

She had fought a wave of disappointment when she'd learned that she wouldn't be working side by side with the laird.

What was she thinking? It was silly, really. Why would she be working with him? They hardly knew each other, and he had already made remarks about them being seen together with no chaperone in sight. She supposed it would bother her if she knew anyone here. But she didn't. She'd heard of the shunning young ladies would be subjected to when the gossip columns wrote about the different compromising scenarios they would find themselves in. She herself had never been the topic of conversation in any of those columns. She'd married Victor without even being introduced into society.

A marriage arranged in a deal between her and Victor's parents. They went through a courtship where Victor presented himself as charming. He had arrived at her doorstep each morning bearing some sort of gift. Flowers. Chocolates. Even jewelry.

She'd been thoroughly fooled. As well as the other girls and women in the city. They oohed and aahed about how lucky she was. If they only knew.

The gifts stopped as soon as they married. And the jewelry he had previously given her, he gathered it all and returned it to the jeweler to get his coin back.

She focused on the ledgers. She didn't need to think about Victor anymore. She'd finally escaped. Lucky for her she just happened to find herself in the company of a very handsome laird. And a kind one.

He also looked like he could crush Victor with a single punch. She couldn't help the smile that played on her lips at the thought.

She sat down at the small wooden desk Gunn had set up for her to work. She settled in but stood up again. If she was to do a thorough job, then she would need to review the ledgers in chronological order. That made the most sense.

Looking at the dates, she organized them from oldest to newest and settled into her seat once again. Pulling down the first ledger from the pile, she opened it to the first page. It was dated September 1810.

Not exactly sure what she was looking for, she scanned the entries, hoping that something would stand out. A pattern. An odd entry. It appeared before the laird left to fight in the war the Thistle & Pig was a thriving and fruitful business. He employed a full staff, including a manager responsible for the pub. The only other person she'd seen since she'd arrived, besides the laird, was Flora. And of course, there was the cook, whom she hadn't seen, but was obviously there.

She wondered where all the staff was now. There was no manager working at the pub when she entered the door the other day.

Reading through the number of liquors that the pub purchased was impressive. She was no expert when it came to such things, but many orders were put through. With so many bottles bought, he had to have the patrons to match. Continuing her review, she read line after line of entries.

Jocelyn became so engrossed in her work that she didn't hear anyone approach and jumped at the sharp knock on the open door frame.

With a little yelp, she jumped and looked up to see Gunn leaning against the door, looking at her curiously. His arms were crossed and the seams of his gray shirt strained from his muscles. Unlike her, gray looked positively dashing on him. He possessed the widest shoulders she'd ever seen in her life. Black trousers hugged his thighs in the most wicked of ways and she had to quickly look away before he caught her gawking.

Swallowing hard, her mouth was suddenly dry.

"Do you need anything?" she asked, wondering why he was standing there.

He pushed off the wall and approached her desk. His massive size filled the small space. "'Tis been some hours since ye started. I wanted to see how ye fared and inquire if ye were hungry."

Had it really already been hours? It seemed like she had just started, but numbers were of great interest to her. She became consumed by them and lost all sense of time. Apparently, that's what had happened here.

She straightened, her back screaming in protest. Stiffly, she tried to stretch out the aches of being hunched over the desk for such an extended amount of time.

Gunn narrowed his eyes. "Mayhap ye have had enough for one day. Why dinna ye join me for tea and sandwiches and ye can tell me all about what ye've uncovered so far."

She rubbed an ache in her neck, trying to ease the tension. "What time is it?"

"'Tis after three."

Her eyebrows shot up in surprise. "Really? The day has seemed to have disappeared on me."

He smiled, the gesture softening the hard planes of his face.

"It seems so. I've had Cook prepare us a light meal to hold us o'er until supper. It should be waiting for us in the dining room."

Standing, she straightened her skirts. "Thank you. It is very thoughtful of you to pay such attention. You needn't worry, however. I would have realized soon enough."

He lifted a brow, a smirk dancing on his lips. "I dinna think e'en ye believe that wee fib that just slipped out of your mouth. Come on. Ye must be ravenous."

Just as he finished speaking her stomach growled loudly, the noise amplified in the small space.

"See." He dipped his head in her direction. "Your belly is giving ye away." He chuckled and spun on his heel, heading down the hall to the dining room she assumed.

Hurrying, she caught up to him. His long strides meant she had to take two steps to his every one to have any semblance of keeping pace with him.

Once they were settled at a table in the dining room, cups of steaming tea were poured, and a servant brought over a tiered tray filled with finger sandwiches.

Jocelyn's stomach rumbled again.

"It appears I saved ye just in time. If I'd waited any longer ye surely would have wilted away at your desk. I canna be blamed for working ye to death. I willna have it." His voice was light, welcoming, and dare she say, held an undertone of flirting.

CHAPTER FOUR

For not the first time since Jocelyn Townsend had walked into his pub, Gunn wondered what the hell he was doing. When he'd come upon her in the room he had arranged to be her work room while she reviewed his ledgers, he was surprised to see how diligently she worked.

She'd given her full concentration to the task and hadn't even heard him walk up.

But when she'd straightened, pain distorting her features, he felt guilty. The urge to go and rub the pain from her muscles was strong and he found himself clenching his fists to stop himself from approaching the lass and doing just that.

Now, as they sat across from each other eating ridiculously small sandwiches that wouldn't appease his appetite in any way, he found himself wanting to engage her in conversation that verged on flirtation. Jesus.

He had asked Cook to set up a tray of sandwiches, but they were to strictly be for Jocelyn. He'd heard from Flora that she hadn't eaten since she'd broken her fast early that morning. She hadn't even left the room.

That worried him. The lass was much too thin to be skipping meals. She needed to plump herself up. Get color into her cheeks that wasn't the fading yellow the bruises left behind.

But once he'd seen her, he didn't want to leave her. So here they were. Nibbling on cucumber sandwiches and drinking tea. He stopped at one. She needed to eat the rest.

"So, tell me, lass. What have ye found? Aught that would explain the pub's and inn's downward trend?"

She chewed daintily, swallowing before answering.

"I started with the ledgers from 1810, so I could get a grasp of what the business looked like when it was thriving. And I must say, you had a thriving business, indeed."

He nodded. "I did. I just dinna ken what happened."

"So far, all is in order. There is naught amiss that would lead me to believe it is a bookkeeping error as of yet. However, I haven't gotten to the point where there has been a downturn in clientele yet."

"Ye are being verra thorough."

"It is the least I could do for you showing me such kindness." She snatched another sandwich and nibbled on the corner, blushing when she noticed him watching her. "These are delicious."

"Ye must remember to eat, lass. I canna have my newest employee fainting from hunger whilst she works." He meant it as a joke, but Jocelyn seemed to close herself off, her shoulders straightening.

"I wouldn't dream of doing such a thing."

"Easy, lass. I jest." He smiled, trying to lighten the mood.

It seemed to work.

"My apologies. I've just, well, I've never had a proper job before obviously. I don't know what exactly is expected."

"Working yourself into a state is most definitely no' what is required or e'en expected. I appreciate your dedication, but not at the expense of your health. Ye look tired. Mayhap after ye finish eating, ye should rest." He wasn't exaggerating. She looked exhausted. Mayhap she was finding the inn's bed lacking and needed one more comfortable. "Is your room to your liking?"

Her head shot up from the cube of sugar she was stirring into her second cup of tea. "Very much so. I cannot offer a complaint about it. It's very nice."

"Are ye sleeping well?"

"As well as can be expected in a new place. Doesn't it always take a few nights to become used to your surroundings?"

Gunn got the feeling there was more to it than what she was saying.

She lowered her eyes and plucked another sandwich off the tray. He was happy to see that she was eating. Mayhap after a few weeks of eating well, she wouldn't look like she would snap in two at the slightest bump.

Though, she was clearly stronger than what outward appearances showed. She survived that beating that she wouldn't admit to. It was possible the journey here was taxing and since she was on her last coin when she arrived, mayhap she couldn't afford meals along the way.

The thought upset him. Were people so cruel to see a starving woman that they couldn't offer her free sustenance? She wouldn't beg for food. That he could tell. She had far too much pride to do that. She was an anomaly. Sometimes she was fierce as a warrior, standing strong, and other times, when she didn't think people were watching, she looked defeated.

He wanted her to be fierce every day. All day. There was naught more enticing than a woman that was confident in herself.

Like when she'd spoken to him about bookkeeping. Her eyes lit up at the subject.

"Would you like more tea?" she asked, drawing his attention back to her.

"Nay. I have had enough. Thank ye." He noticed her eyeing the last remaining sandwich on the tray.

"Go on, lass. That last sandwich is calling your name."

In a flash she reached out and snatched the sandwich.

A laugh burst from his chest.

A comely blush dusted her freckled cheeks. "I'm sorry."

"Nay, I like a woman that kens what she wants," he jested, but even to his own ears, the double entendre was too much.

Her eyes flared wide.

He needed to steer the conversation in another direction. "I can have Cook prepare some more if ye are still hungry?"

Shaking her head, she flattened her palms on her stomach. "Oh no. I couldn't eat another bite."

"Well, I dinna ken what Cook has on the menu for supper tonight, but I am sure ye will find it delicious."

"I've no doubt. She is most adept."

"Thank ye." He leaned in conspiratorially. "I stole her from another establishment."

Jocelyn sucked in a breath. "Truly?"

"Aye. Her food was so divine I wanted to it eat e'ery day. She also was one of the reasons people frequented the Thistle & Pig. No' so much anymore, mind ye. But once upon a time, she was."

He only hoped he wouldn't have to let her go and replace her with someone less experienced and lacking in skills.

"If ye are set, I am going to go o'er to the pub side and see how the e'ening is shaping up."

She smiled, the gesture transforming her face, lighting up her light blue eyes. She was a bonny lass.

"I am fine. Thank ye for the company."

He stood and gave her a slight bow. "If ye need aught, I will be there."

A few people occupied tables in the pub. Gunn approached the bar to speak with Thomas. "How's the day faring so far, Thomas?"

Running a towel along the polished wood, the man shrugged. "We've had a few people in and out all afternoon."

Gunn pushed a hand through his hair, scratching his scalp and let out a long breath. "If it doesna improve, go ahead and close up early. Nay use staying for an empty pub."

He left the pub and made his way to his study, praying for a miracle.

After Jocelyn had finished her third cup of tea, she finally left the dining room, her belly full and satisfied. She hadn't realized how hungry she had been until the tray of delectable sandwiches had been placed in between her and Gunn.

She was quite certain he had only eaten one, mayhap two, sandwiches. Definitely no more than two. For such a large man, he needed more sustenance than that. He was being kind letting her have her fill. Embarrassing as it was now that she thought about it. He must think her lacking in manners for her to be so uncultured.

But she had to keep in mind the babe growing in her belly. Feeding it well was a priority so that she could birth a healthy babe.

Tempted to return to her desk to continue reading through the ledgers, she wondered if that would anger him. He'd told her to stop for the day.

But there were still hours left until the evening meal.

Moving to the window, she looked out at the sky. The sun wasn't shining, but the bright and puffy clouds didn't threaten rain.

Grabbing her bonnet from the chair, she brought it over her head, tucking wayward wisps of hair into the sides, and tied it into a bow at her neck. With her reticule looped over her wrist, she wrapped her cloak around her shoulders. It was time to finish exploring the part of town that she hadn't seen the other day.

"Going out, miss?" Flora asked as she passed her downstairs.

"I won't be gone long. I just want to familiarize myself with the town."

The girl dipped into a curtsy and continued on her way.

Outside, the air was crisp. Jocelyn drew in a deep breath, filling her lungs with the clean air. Scents were different here than in Rochester. Rochester seemed so much dirtier. Unkempt. Crowded. When she walked the streets there, people were always around. It didn't matter the street. The time. The day. There were always people everywhere.

But here, the streets were quiet. Sure, there were people, but they were far and few between. They smiled cheerily at her as they passed.

She went in the opposite direction of where she had gone last time. On this side, there was a bank and a tailor. She passed a mercantile. Curious, she entered, a bell at the top of the door announcing her entry. A cheery man with a welcoming smile greeted her.

"I dinna ken I've seen ye around here. Welcome. Are ye new in town?"

"I am."

"Well, if there is aught ye need or are looking for, give me a holler. If I dinna have it in store, I can try to procure it for ye."

She dipped her head in thanks. "That is most kind of you."

Was everyone in this town so nice? She hadn't met one person with an ill personality. She browsed the shelves of sweet treats and colorful candies that made her mouth water even though she'd just had her fill of finger sandwiches.

On another shelf were kitchen essentials. Flour, sugar, lard, molasses. Other items that one would use to make a meal.

Another shelf held personal items. Soaps scented with different herbs and spices. Lifting a bar scented with cinnamon to her nose, she breathed in deeply, closing her eyes. The smell reminding her of the morning buns the cook from her childhood used to make.

"Smells lovely doesna it?"

Nodding, she returned it to its space.

"My wife has me keep those in stock. They're her favorite."

She smiled. "Thank you for letting me look around. You have a wonderful day."

He dipped his head. "Dinna forget. I'm here for all your needs."

She waved goodbye and stepped outside. Next to the mercantile was a jeweler. She didn't even pause at the window that boasted all things shiny and expensive. Unable to afford anything at the mercantile, she surely couldn't afford anything in there.

Besides, she had no need for baubles. She had much more important things to spend her money on.

Like her babe. How was she going to be able to raise a child on her own? She had no husband. Or at least one she never wanted to see again. No home. Certainly, she couldn't remain living in her room at the Thistle & Pig. That was no type of environment for a child.

It wasn't the first time she wondered about her future, nor would it be her last. But most important of all was finding a safe place to live and raise the babe.

And what of Gunn? What would he do when he realized she was with child? She came upon a bench and sat down, pondering her situation. Would he put her out on the street? What would she do then?

She might have to live in the tenements. She shuddered at the thought, but it would still be better than giving Victor access to her babe. The worry she felt over what he could do to an innocent being turned her stomach.

A couple passed by, smiling at her as they continued on their walk. A surge of longing tugged at her heart. They looked so happy. She wanted that. Wanted someone that would look at her the way that man looked at his wife as they strolled together, enjoying the evening.

Sighing, she pushed off the bench. She should head back to the inn.

"Good eve, miss." A man addressed her as he approached. He was slight of stature but had a friendly face.

"Hello," she answered, but as she moved to walk, he stepped in front of her.

"Where are ye walking? Let me escort ye." He jutted a bony elbow out in her direction. "A lass as bonny as ye shouldna be walking alone."

She smiled nervously. "I'm fine. Thank you." She clutched her cloak tighter around her shoulders and moved to sidestep the man.

For reasons unknown, he once again stepped in front of her.

"Sir. Excuse me. I have someplace I must be."

"Come on now, surely ye could use the company."

She was just bunching her hand into a fist when the man stepped back.

"I believe the lady asked ye to let her be," a familiar voice sounded from over her shoulder, the deep baritone enveloping her in a warm embrace.

Gunn.

Relief washed over her.

"Sir Burnett." A wave of panic flashed in the man's eyes. "I was just offering the lady an escort home."

"And she politely said nay. That was your hint to leave."

The two men stood there as if they were squaring off, Gunn towering over the other man, and nearly twice as wide. Jocelyn noticed Gunn's clenched fists. It looked like he was willing to pull punches if need be. She had been, too.

She was both appalled and grateful. The thought of him getting into fisticuffs for her was upsetting.

Finally, the man bowed. "I shall be on my way. Remember, the streets are no' safe for a lady to walk alone," he sneered. It sounded like he was warning her. "I bid ye a good eve."

Setting a hand on Gunn's arm, his shoulders relaxed, his fists unclenching. "Thank ye. He was very persistent."

"Aye." Concern furrowed Gunn's eyes. "The streets are safe, dinna believe a word he says. Howe'er, I would suggest if ye plan to walk, ye shouldna do so alone."

"I was just on my way back. I will take your suggestion into consideration, however, as you know, you and Flora are the only people I know here. It appears I will be walking alone when I want to go out."

"Ye willna."

"Pardon?"

He seemed to realize she felt affronted at his out-of-bound step and backed off, pushing a hand through his hair, making the short strands stand on end. It was an enticing look on him.

"I apologize. I have nay right to tell ye what to do." He blew out a breath. "As ye can see, I am much better at dealing with men. On the morrow, my good friend Malcolm will be visiting with his wife, Lizzie. Mayhap the two of ye can spend some time together."

"That is very kind of you. I would like that."

Gunn smiled sheepishly and held his arm out. "Allow me to walk ye home?"

Home. She liked the sound of that.

She nodded and slipped her arm into the crook of his elbow, letting the heat emanating through his coat warm her.

As they walked, she was reminded of the couple she'd seen before, imagining that was how they appeared to people they passed on their way back to the inn.

Once inside the inn, Gunn quickly excused himself, leaving Jocelyn confused at the two sides of him that he'd shown her. He had the gruff side, the one that when it came to the stranger on the street, looked positively lethal. But then he'd also shown her a softer, kinder side. One where he was sweet and caring.

And she was finding the more time she spent with the man, the more she enjoyed it. The more she wanted to explore all sides of him.

CHAPTER FIVE

GUNN HAD DONE his best to steer clear of Jocelyn since they'd arrived back at the inn the night before.

He found himself caring too much. Consumed with thoughts of what would have happened if he hadn't come upon her when he did. Of course, it was possible the man was truly being chivalrous, but his insistence led Gunn to believe otherwise.

Today, he'd kept busy in the pub, taking inventory, stacking cases. Any attempt to keep his mind off Jocelyn. He didn't ken why he cared so much. He didn't even ken her.

But the pull to check in on her while she worked to ensure she ate was strong. He slammed a crate onto the stack.

"Sir?" Thomas asked, his eyebrows furrowed.

"Aye?"

"Ye're going to obliterate the contents if ye keep banging the crates about as ye are. We dinna sell enough liquor to be losing it to broken bottles."

Gunn bit the inside of his cheek. Thomas wasn't wrong. They needed all the inventory they had to remain intact.

"Pour me a whisky, will ye," he said sharply and approached the bar.

Thomas remained silent as he filled a glass and pushed it toward Gunn.

"I apologize. I didna mean to snap."

Thomas shrugged. "We've all got things we are working through," he said as he turned and replaced the bottle of whisky on the shelf.

The door opened and a few men entered. Gunn had seen them around but didn't ken their names. They sat at a table by the window, deep in conversation, before gesturing for Thomas to take their orders.

It wasn't really his job. But, just as he had cut back on Theodore's and Thomas's hours, he'd had to let his two server girls go.

"Ye have things handled in here?" Gunn asked when Thomas came back.

"Aye. All is under control."

Gunn gave him a nod and left the pub in search of Flora. If anyone kenned if Jocelyn had eaten yet, it was her. The young woman managed to be everywhere all at once. If anyone wanted to ken what was happening in the inn, all they had to do was ask Flora.

He found her covered in flour up to her elbows helping Cook knead bread in the kitchen.

"My laird," she said and a puff of flour floated through the air as she dipped into a curtsy.

"Flora, has Miss Townsend eaten today? Other than when she broke her fast," he quickly added when she opened her mouth to answer.

"Nay, my laird. Not that I've seen."

"Cook, do ye have some sustenance I can take to her before she collapses at her desk?"

The cook nodded and went about putting a plate together.

"That's nearly what she did yesterday. I willna have her doing it again today." He admired her dedication to her work, but he didn't want it to be at a detriment to her health.

"I can bring her the meal, my laird," Flora offered.

He should accept the offer. To keep his distance from the woman that was occupying way too many of his mind's thoughts.

"Nay. I prefer to bring it to her myself. Thank ye, Flora."

Cook handed him a plate piled high with dried meats, fruit, and bread. It was as if she too believed the lass needed to eat heartily.

He smiled his thanks and left the kitchen.

But when he knocked on the open door, Jocelyn wasn't there. Frowning, he entered the room and set the plate on a pile of crates. Looking at the ledger on the desk, she had been here working. There were handwritten notes on a piece of parchment paper beside the book. He noted her neat, delicate penmanship. The swooping curves in the words revealed her delicate femininity.

Where could she have gone?

That's when he heard it. It sounded like she was retching. He hurried out of the room and around the corner. There was a door that led out into the small garden. The door was slightly ajar, and he could hear her getting sick again.

Rushing forward, he burst through the door. "Lass?"

She jumped, straightening quickly, swiping at her mouth with the back of her hand. "Sir. I was just going back inside to continue working."

As she moved to pass him, he reached out his hand, grasping her upper arm gently. "Are ye ill?" he asked, concern lacing his voice.

"Oh, no. I am fine. I promise."

He looked at the evidence on the ground that said otherwise.

"I demand ye to be truthful with me, lass. I heard ye retching. Have ye eaten?"

She blanched, her face losing what little color it had left, and she clasped her stomach. "I am not hungry. I ate this morn."

"That was hours ago. I brought ye food."

She pressed her lips together and shook her head. "I really cannot. I fear my stomach is unsettled."

"Should I have Cook make ye a broth of some sort? A light soup, mayhap."

She smiled, but it was forced. "I, no. She is busy enough, as are we all. I will just wait for my stomach to cease its churning and then will sup."

He wasn't convinced she was speaking truthfully.

"I promise. I will eat when I am able." She took a deep breath. "I feel better already."

"Are ye being forthright?"

She chuckled. "Of course. I must have just eaten something that didn't settle well earlier. I will be fine in a bit." Her eyes lit up. "I want to show you something."

Allowing her to change the subject, he followed her to her desk where she stood in front of an open ledger and pointed to an entry. "Do you see this?"

He bent and read the line where her finger rested. There was no transaction title, but a comely amount was withdrawn from the coffers.

"Do you know what this was for? I cannot account for it with any corresponding order or receipt."

"I dinna ken." He looked at the writing. It was Theodore's.

"That is not the only one." She flipped to a previous page. "Here." She pointed to another entry.

He read the entry, again, no transaction, but a hefty amount had been withdrawn. Also in Theodore's script.

"And here." She pointed to another page and Gunn couldn't believe what he was seeing.

"When did these start?"

"The beginning of February 1812."

That was when he was away. Serving the country. Was Theodore skimming off of his business while he fought? Would he really do that? Was he the cause of his business failing?

Nay. He refused to believe it. Even so, that still wouldn't explain why people had stopped coming to the pub. Or the inn.

There had to be something more.

"Can you keep a listing of all similar entries along with the dates and amounts?"

She held up a piece of parchment paper and smiled. "Already have. I thought you might find them of interest."

"I do. Aye. Good work. But ye've worked enough for the day. Go freshen up."

Surprisingly, she didn't fight with him to work longer.

Sticking the paper in the ledger as a placeholder, she closed the book.

"My friend and his wife should be arriving soon. I would love it if ye would join us for dinner this eve." He was treading a thin line. She essentially was his employee. Someone he had hired to work for him. Mixing work and pleasure was never a good idea.

"Are you sure?" she asked uncertainly.

Was he?

"Aye. I believe ye and Lizzie will become fast friends." What the hell was he saying?

"If you insist. I don't want to intrude."

"Ye canna intrude when ye've been invited, lass."

She smiled. "I will see you at dinner then. Thank you."

As she passed, he handed her the plate of food. "Ye dinna have to eat it now, but in case ye get hungry before dinner."

He watched her walk out of the small room, then fixed his gaze on the ledgers. Anger welled up inside of him. If Theodore was truly the cause of his business failing, he didn't ken what he would do. Gunn had entrusted the businesses to him whilst he was away. Believed he was trustworthy.

The more he thought on it, the more he couldn't fathom why he would do such a thing.

But if he found out he was indeed the cause. The man better run for if Gunn got a hold of him, he'd wish he'd never crossed him.

JOCELYN WISHED SHE had a different colored gown to attend dinner with Gunn and his friends. The gray was fine while she was working, but to entertain guests? It was not worthy of that.

Never mind that the style was woefully out of fashion.

She laughed out loud in her room. Listen to yourself. Entertain guests. As if they were her own.

No, Gunn was just showing kindness by inviting her to join them.

A knock sounded and Flora announced herself. "Miss? May I come in?"

"Yes, please."

She was relieved to see the young girl. Mayhap she could help her look more presentable and worthy of dining with the laird and his friends.

Oh no. A new thought entered her mind. Was his friend a laird as well? Or something more. Oh dear. She would appear dreadfully underdressed.

"What is it, miss? Ye look as if ye've seen a ghost."

"As I'm sure you know, I'm to meet the laird for dinner tonight, along with his friend and his friend's wife."

Flora nodded. "Aye, the earl."

"Pardon?" She gulped.

"Aye. Malcolm Kennedy, the earl of Cassilis. He's verra nice. His wife as well. Ye will like her." She paused, her brows drawn down. "Are ye well, miss?"

Jocelyn threw her hands up in frustration. "How am I to meet people of such high-standing when all I have is drab, gray gowns? They are certainly not made for high society."

Flora shushed her. "Ye needna worry. They arena like that. Your gowns are fine. Quality made."

"But they are ugly."

"Hmmm." Flora cocked her hip to the side and scratched her chin. "I may have a solution. There is a chest downstairs in storage that has gowns in it."

"Why would the laird have a chest full of gowns?"

Flora giggled. "They arena his, obviously. But things get left behind, either on purpose or by accident. It doesna make sense to throw them away. Let me check to see if one might be fitting for ye for dinner." She spun and rushed out of the room before Jocelyn could tell her not to go through any trouble.

But she was gone. Intent on her mission.

Jocelyn sat at the vanity and pinched her cheeks, trying to get color into them. It was no use. Her usually pale skin wouldn't hold any color other than the faint yellow that was left from her bruises.

Mayhap Flora had access to some cosmetics she could borrow. She shook her head. That may be a bit too much to ask for.

Picking up the brush, she ran it through her hair, continuing with long strokes until it shone under the lantern light. Then she pinned it into her usual chignon at the base of her neck. She should probably try a different style, but honestly, it was the only one she was comfortable doing. It was the same way Victor had insisted she wore her hair. Simple, naught fancy.

That alone made her want to change the style.

Frustrated, she pulled the pins out and let her hair topple over her shoulders. It had a slight wave to it, with streaks of honey mixed throughout the blonde.

Flora returned, her arms carrying multiple gowns and she paused.

"Your hair is beautiful."

Jocelyn felt her cheeks heat at the compliment. "Thank you. I wish I knew how to style it properly."

"Well, let us find ye a dress that fits and mayhap I can help ye with that. I canna promise 'twill be perfect, but I can try."

"It's a deal," she said happily and hopped up to look at the dresses Flora was laying out on the bed. They were all gorgeous gowns. "Women left these behind?" She asked in astonishment. "I couldn't imagine doing such a thing."

"Ye'd be surprised the things that get left behind. Gowns, shirts. Shoes, slippers. Hair pins, barrettes. All sorts of baubles."

"That is amazing." Jocelyn ran her hands down a gold-colored gown, with a green sash. The satin was butter soft to the touch.

"That would complement ye well. 'Twill bring out the honey streaks in your hair." She lifted it up and shook it out. "This one was left recently." She gave it a sniff. "It doesna smell as if it has been closed up. There isna any mustiness to it. Let me help ye get it on. I believe 'twill fit."

Once Flora fastened the last button, Jocelyn moved to the looking glass. The gown was a little big on her small frame, but it still looked better than her gray gowns.

"Ye look beautiful."

"Thank ye. I will pay ye for it when I receive my first payout."

"Pfft." Flora waved a hand in front of her in dismissal. "Ye will do nay such thing. 'Tis no' my gown. As I said, someone left it. 'Tis yours now. Ye can do with it as ye please. If we had more time, we could have brought it to the modiste to have her take it in, but I think in a pinch 'twill work well. What do ye think?"

"It's very nice." She ran her hands over the satin. "And so soft." It had been a long time since Jocelyn had felt so pretty.

Flora finished tying the sash into a pretty bow at her waist. "Now, sit, and let's get your hair styled. Remember, 'tis no' my area of expertise, but I will try."

Jocelyn laughed. It was hard not to be happy in Flora's presence. She was so cheerful, it was contagious. She sat in the chair as Flora brushed, pulled, tied, and pinned. By the time she was done, Jocelyn almost didn't recognize herself.

Flora had pinned her hair in soft waves that piled high on her head, with soft curls that fell over her ears. She'd fastened a jewel-encrusted barrette in the center.

Stepping back, she studied her work and smiled. "Well, it took a while, and I'm no ladies maid, but I must say I think I did a fair good job of it."

"You definitely did. I can't remember a time when I've had my hair styled so nice." And she couldn't. Her wedding day, mayhap.

No, not even then.

"The laird is going to have a hard time keeping his eyes off of ye."

"I don't know about that," she said shyly, dipping her head to hide her blush.

"Mark my words, he will. He may seem gruff on the outside, but he's actually quite nice."

She'd noticed, but she wasn't about to admit that to Flora.

She almost didn't want to admit it to herself.

CHAPTER SIX

"Is there any whisky in this establishment or shall we go elsewhere?" a loud voice called from the doorway of the Thistle & Pig.

Gunn smiled at the voice he would recognize anywhere and turned to greet one of his best friends and his wife.

"Malcolm. 'Tis great to see ye, brother."

They closed the distance and clasped in an embrace.

"'Tis been too long."

"Well, ye've been busy acclimating to married life. How's it treating ye?" Gunn clapped Malcolm on the back. "Speaking of which, where's Lizzie? Dinna tell me ye have frightened her off already," he jested.

"Nay, she will be in shortly. After being closed up in the carriage all day, she wanted to enjoy the fresh air for a few minutes."

As if on cue, the door opened, and Malcolm's wife, Lizzie, walked in.

"'Tis lo'ely to see ye again, Lizzie." He bent and kissed her hand.

"Keep your lips off my wife, Burnett," Malcolm growled, but his mouth tipped up into a smile.

Lizzie laughed. "Ignore him. He gets cranky when he hasna eaten. How are ye, Gunn?" She reached up on her tiptoes and kissed his cheek. "Ye look well."

Gunn harrumphed at her attention.

Lizzie looped her arms around Malcolm's waist and squeezed.

"Dinna give Gunn such a hard time. He works hard."

"Thank ye, Lizzie. Ye both must be hungry. I've had Cook prepare a meal. I've also invited someone else to join us, if ye dinna mind."

Lizzie tilted her head as she studied his face, her eyes narrowing. "Ye've invited a lady to join us," she stated with awe.

"Nay. No' Gunn," Malcolm chimed in. "He will be fore'er single. The eternal bachelor."

Gunn sneered at Malcolm. "Since we are in the company of a lady, I willna say what I'm thinking. But Lizzie is correct. I have invited a lady to join us."

"Do tell," Lizzie drawled.

"She's new in town and needs a friend. I believe ye two will get on well. I'd appreciate it if ye would give her a chance."

"Of course. I would love to meet her."

"Splendid. She will be down shortly. Shall we make our way to the dining room?" Gunn waved his palm in the direction that would lead them out of the pub and into the inn.

Lizzie started walking and then spun around, holding her hand up. "One minute. Ye said she will be down. Is she staying at the inn?"

"Good catch, love." Malcolm nuzzled her neck.

"How are ye two still like this?"

Malcolm chuckled. "We havena been married *that* long."

"Dinna dodge my question, Gunn. She's here?"

"Aye. She arrived several nights ago." His brows furrowed with concern.

"I ken that look. Is there something amiss with her?" Malcolm inquired.

"She's lovely. Sweet natured, but strong. She has her secrets. That's what I want to talk to ye about after dinner."

Lizzie was looking at him, her head cocked to the side as she listened to him talk.

"Ye are interested in her." Her eyebrows shot up.

"I am no'," he snapped. Too quickly, and Lizzie picked up on it straightaway.

"Is it happening? Can it be true?" She jested in a sing-song voice.

"What are ye yammering about? Let us go eat." He tried pushing them toward the inn, but Lizzie stood her ground and crossed her arms.

"Oh my, 'tis." She clapped her hands together, happily.

"Now I am confused," Malcolm grunted. "What is happening?"

"Gunn has finally found the woman that's going to sweep him off his feet."

Malcolm gave her a look of disbelief and then steered his wife to the door that would lead them to the inn.

Gunn held back for a few moments. Was Lizzie right? Was she seeing something that he wasn't? Sure, he found Jocelyn intriguing. She was beautiful, smart, strong. Independent.

He groaned, pushing his hand through his hair.

Lizzie was right. Damn her.

GUNN, MALCOLM, AND Lizzie had just sat down at the table when Jocelyn appeared in the doorway. He sucked in his breath at the sight before him.

Standing there like an angel sent from the heavens, wrapped in gold, with a shy smile on her beautiful face.

He stood so quickly to welcome her that his chair nearly toppled over.

"Jocelyn, welcome."

Her cheeks flushed. "I apologize. It appears I am late."

"Nay no' at all. We just sat down. Please." Gunn pulled out the chair next to him for her to take a seat.

Malcolm stood as well.

Once she was seated, Gunn made the introductions. "Jocelyn, I'd like ye to meet my good friend, Malcolm, and his wife Lizzie."

"Lovely to meet ye, lass," Malcolm greeted.

Lizzie covered Jocelyn's hand with hers. "Finally, another woman to talk to whilst we visit. We will have to share a drink after dinner. Ye are English, are ye no'? I would love to hear all about it."

Gunn breathed a sigh of relief. Lizzie's outgoing personality drew Jocelyn in from the start and he was grateful.

"Thank ye," he mouthed at his best friend's wife.

She gave a slight nod of her head and turned her attention back to Jocelyn. As they got lost in conversation, Gunn turned his attention back to Malcolm.

"How's business?" Malcolm asked, looking around the empty dining room.

"Ye have to ask?" Gunn answered with defeat.

Malcolm chuckled, then grew serious. "What's happened and is this just a recent turn?"

Gunn palmed his face. "Honestly, I dinna ken. All was well when I left. But I came back to my coffers drained, and hardly any patrons. And they havena returned."

"Is that what ye need me to look into? I'll figure it out."

"Nay, 'tis no' that. Jocelyn is actually helping me with that piece."

Malcolm raised a brow in question. "How so?" His eyes darted to Jocelyn and then back to Gunn.

Would ye believe me if I told ye she was a bookkeeper?"

Malcolm's eyes slid over to Jocelyn again and Gunn could tell he was sizing her up before shaking his head. "Nay. I wouldna believe it."

"She is. Taught by her father. So she says," he added.

Flora entered, pushing a cart filled with dome-covered plates, to serve dinner, setting a plate in front of each of them.

Malcolm hummed in appreciation. "Your cook is still here, I see. I look forward to her food e'ery visit."

Scents of roast duck, boiled carrots, and parsnip mash filled the room.

"This looks delicious and smells divine," Jocelyn cooed. "Flora, give my regards to Cook, please."

"Of course, my lady." She curtsied, then refilled their wine glasses before returning to the kitchen.

Conversation flowed easily over dinner. Gunn was pleased to see Jocelyn and Lizzie getting on well. He had no doubt it would be so. Everyone was Lizzie's friend, and Jocelyn looked like she could desperately use a confidant. He was happy to bring them together.

Dessert consisted of egg custard with a berry compote, once again, cooked to perfection. Jocelyn took a bite and moaned, closing her eyes as she savored the sweet treat. She opened her eyes and caught Gunn staring.

With a hand over her mouth, she giggled.

"I can't help it. I could eat like this every day and be in heaven."

Gunn suddenly yearned to be the one to ensure she could enjoy meals like this every day.

Malcolm shot him a look of awareness, but Gunn shook his head. Trying to tell his friend he was reading more into the situation than what was there.

But inside he kenned it was a lie.

The more time he spent in Jocelyn's company, the more he wanted to ken her better.

"So, how did ye come to be at the Thistle & Pig?" Lizzie asked after dinner and she and Jocelyn had settled into a room that had a roaring fire and comfortable chairs to relax in.

"It was a journey," she answered, taking a sip of sherry.

It looked like Lizzie was waiting for her to expand her answer and when she didn't, instead of prying, she moved on to more neutral conversation.

"Did I overhear Gunn saying that ye were doing some bookkeeping work for him?"

She bobbed her head up and down. "Yes, though I am not so certain he is happy with my findings so far."

"Nay? Why no'?"

Jocelyn sighed, wondering if she should divulge such information to Lizzie. It appeared that Gunn trusted her as Malcolm's wife. And of course, he trusted Malcolm wholeheartedly. "I fear I have uncovered an unsavory plot that includes money being stolen from Gunn's coffers," she said quietly.

"Nay," Lizzie exclaimed.

"Unfortunately, yes. It seems to have started around a year or so after he left to fight in the war. Transactions for large amounts of money, but no inventory acquired."

Lizzie shook her head and took a sip of sherry. "Wow. 'Tis impressive ye uncovered that. And that ye bookkeep. Where'er did ye learn such a skill?"

She smiled wistfully. She only had good memories when it came to her parents. "My father. When I was young, he wanted me to be able to keep track of the household I would one day be responsible for." Thoughts of Victor entered her mind, but she quickly willed them away.

"And did ye?" Lizzie asked.

"Did I what?"

"Keep your eye on the books? Or have ye no household to oversee yet?"

Jocelyn shifted in her seat, and took a sip of sherry as she pondered her answer. "I did have a household, yes. However, I was not allowed access to the books."

Lizzie frowned. "Why e'er no'? 'Twas your house, aye?"

Jocelyn pressed her lips together as she stared into the flames, watching them twist and turn violently together. It reminded her of the violent fights she would have with Victor.

Leaning over, Lizzie patted her arm. "I'm sorry. Ye have no need to answer my prying questions." She laughed. "Malcolm says I get carried away and ask too much."

Jocelyn smiled. "It's not that. I-I'm just not ready to talk about some things yet."

"Say no more. Let's move to more pleasant conversation. "What do ye think of Gunn?"

Jocelyn choked on the sip of sherry she just took, making her cough and sputter, as she tried to catch her breath.

Lizzie hurried over to her, patting her on the back. "Are ye well? Gunn will no' be happy if he finds out I killed ye from choking."

Jocelyn heaved in a shaky breath and smirked. "Excuse me for that. I must have swallowed wrong."

"Hmmm. I think it had more to do with the question I asked. I saw the stolen looks between ye two o'er dinner."

Jocelyn scoffed. "Whatever are you talking about?" But she knew what Lizzie asked about. Though she didn't think they were being obvious. Apparently, they were.

"Ye ken exactly what I speak of, but 'tis fine. I will leave the subject alone for now. Though, he is handsome, is he no'?"

"You have a husband," Jocelyn said quietly, looking around the room to make sure no one had entered and overheard their conversation.

"I do. And I must say, in his group of friends, there isna an unattractive one in the bunch. All five of them are handsome. Caring. And love hard. Gunn is no exception."

She did agree that Malcolm was handsome. Not as much as Gunn. Gunn's gruff exterior and teddy bear interior appealed to her. For what reason, she couldn't comprehend. Someone who looked perpetually irked wasn't someone that she would normally find attractive, but for Gunn, it worked. Mayhap because she kept seeing glimpses of the kind and caring man break through his gruffness.

Lizzie waggled a finger at her. "I see ye thinking about it. I canna blame ye one bit. Gunn is a great man. He deserves a great woman in his life. He's long overdue."

With a sigh, Jocelyn crossed her legs. "I don't think I can be the woman that he needs."

"Balderdash," Lizzie blurted. "As I said, I saw the looks. Malcolm, too. If he had no interest in ye, he wouldna have invited ye to join us for dinner. One thing about Gunn, he's pig-headed. Stubborn. Ne'er wants to admit to aught. No' e'en to himself. His tell is in his gestures. So him asking ye to dinner? That was a big step for him."

"I, I don't know what to say."

"Ye needna say aught. Just keep watching him and the things he does. That will tell ye e'erything ye need to ken."

Would it? Jocelyn wasn't sure. Of course, Gunn had been nothing but kind to her, but kindness didn't mean anything more than that. Lizzie herself said he was a nice man. A caring man. His actions so far just seemed to fall in line with his personality.

"Och, has he asked ye to join him on holiday?" Lizzie asked. "Gunn handed us an invite to spend some time at his home. He invited his other friends and their families as well."

"Gunn doesn't live here?" She was confused.

Lizzie laughed. "Nay, of course no'. He has a home. A castle actually." She cocked her head to the side. "Has he not been back home since ye've arrived?" She nodded her head slowly. "See, I told ye. He has his own way of showing his feelings."

"I don't know where he has been staying at night. Just that I have seen him every day since I came to town. Both early in the morn and late at night. So, I just assumed he lived here."

"He owns multiple houses. He has a country house as well."

Jocelyn thought about that. If he had so many homes, why the concern over the pub and inn. Granted, she realized that no one wanted to be stolen from. But she was under the assumption that if he didn't turn the pub and inn around, that he would lose everything. Obviously, that wasn't the case.

"I had no idea. But, also, no. He hasn't asked me anywhere."

"I've a feeling it will come about shortly."

Jocelyn chuckled. "You seem to have a good understanding of Gunn."

"Wait until ye meet e'eryone else. All of us wives understand them better than they understand themselves."

"You've met them all?"

"Och, aye. Ye will like them. There's Gwen who is married to Nicholas. Clarissa who is married to Alexander, and Willamina, who's married to Finlay. All of them are busy making bairns and raising wee ones, which is lovely to see. 'Tis been awhile since we've all been together under one roof, so the gathering is long overdue."

She would have to make note of the names and try to remember them all. She scoffed. What was she thinking? Why would she need to know all of their names? It had nothing to do with her.

"I'm actually surprised the invite came from Gunn. In the time I have kenned e'eryone, we've ne'er gathered at Gunn's house." She leaned into Jocelyn. "See? Just one more thing he's doing out of the ordinary. Because of ye."

Shaking her head, Jocelyn reminded Lizzie that she had not been invited.

"No' yet," she stated in a singsong voice. "But ye will be. I'd bet my right hand on it."

Could it be? Did she want it to be? Did she want an invite? When she'd left Victor, she had no direction. No person that cared for her.

Once she'd arrived here, she'd immediately got the feeling that she'd arrived home. It was odd and didn't make sense, but it was true.

She felt more at home here in the short time she'd been here than the whole time she'd lived with Victor.

And that said so much.

CHAPTER SEVEN

"I NEED A favor," Gunn proclaimed, once he and Malcolm settled in the pub, glasses of whisky on the table and lit pipes in their hands. Swirls of cherry smoke floating above their heads.

"Whate'er ye need. I'm your man."

"'Tis about Jocelyn."

Malcolm barked out a laugh. "Nay, I couldna have guessed that."

"Funny."

"Ye are enamored with the lass."

It wasn't a question.

"I am no'," Gunn said nonchalantly, trying to throw Malcolm off of the feelings Jocelyn was bringing to the surface.

"Ye forget who ye are talking to. 'Tis plain as day. And obvious o'er dinner. Ye couldna stop your eyes from wandering o'er to her throughout the meal."

"Mayhap."

Malcolm puffed on his cigar and blew out a series of small smoke rings, where they loftily floated through the air, widening before finally dissolving. "She's bonny. Seems smart."

"Verra."

"Alright. I'll leave ye to your delusions that ye have no interest in the lady." He sat up in his chair. "Back to business. What do ye need?"

"I want to ken her background. Where she's from. What happenstance led to her arriving here, alone. No husband. No chaperone."

"She seems old enough to get away without a chaperone. Widow mayhap?"

Gunn nodded. "The thought crossed my mind. When she arrived, she was nursing bruises. They were fading, so they had happened quite some time before, but she was definitely beaten." He shook his head, clenching his jaw. "She gave me a tall tale of being clumsy and running into a door. All those bruises? Nay. There was no chance that was the source. If ye look closely ye can still see some of them, though she tries to hide them."

"Did ye tell her ye didna believe her?"

Gunn traced a rivet in the wooden tabletop with the tip of his finger. "Nay, I didna want to scare her away. Her eyes when she arrived were weary. And she was so thin. And broke."

"So ye gave her a job, a place to stay, and meals?"

Gunn bobbed his head from side to side. "Aye and nay. She wanted to pay for the room, but I just couldna in good conscience let her pay full price. She had mayhap two coins. I wasna about to take her last coins. So, I offered her the room at a discount. I didna think she would appreciate it to be free."

"That makes sense. What about the meals and the job?"

"As I said, she was far too slim. She looked liked she'd missed more than one meal. I threw the meals in with the cost of the room."

Malcolm laughed. "So those were free."

"Nay. I told her they were included with the room."

"But they arena."

"Aye, but she doesna need to ken that. She approached me the next day for employment. It wasna something I was e'en contemplating. But she said she was in desperate need of work. Out of her offers, she mentioned that she kenned books and ledgers. Numbers. Ye've seen the state of my business. I've needed to go through the books for a long time to figure out what has happened to it. I gave the task to her and told her I'd include room and board—and pay her a salary."

Malcolm's brows shot up. "Really? Ye do have it bad."

"I doona. I dinna want to see her suffer any further. She'd obviously already had a rough go of it. I didna want to add to her burdens."

"So instead ye added to your own?" Malcolm continued when Gunn didn't answer. "All right. What information do ye have for me to go on?" Malcolm pulled out a small piece of paper he always kept on him and a charcoal pencil.

"Her last name is Townsend and she hails from Rochester. I dinna believe that's where she was born, but that's where she was living when she left. And her father's surname is Bixby."

"Tis no' much but hopefully 'twill be enough for me to find out something."

"I appreciate that."

Malcolm's forehead creased as he thought of something.

"Did she find aught in your ledgers?"

Gunn sighed. He still wasn't ready to accept the fact that his longtime employee, and someone he had considered a friend, may be stealing from him.

"Aye."

"Care to share? It looks like it has ye conflicted."

He took a puff from his pipe, held the smoke in his lungs before exhaling. "I think Theodore may be stealing from me."

"What? He's been with ye for years."

"Aye. That's what makes it so hard to swallow. 'Tis something I ne'er would have expected from him."

"How are ye planning on handling him?"

Gunn shrugged. "I dinna ken yet. I want Jocelyn to complete her review, so I have all the details and times."

"Ye're just going to let him continue working? What if he steals more?"

Barking out a laugh, Gunn shook his head. "There isna anymore to take."

"'Tis that bad?" Malcolm asked, concern furrowing his brow.

"Aye."

They sat in silence for a few long moments, enjoying their pipes and whisky.

"We got your invitation to gather at your estate in the coming weeks." Malcolm finally spoke. "First time to gather at your place. With all of us, anyhow. Was that spurned by a certain bonny lass?" he inquired teasingly.

Rolling his eyes, Gunn puffed on his pipe. "Nay." But even as he spoke the word he kenned it was a lie. He found himself craving family. As his friends married one by one with bairns for some of them following shortly after, he longed for that. When Jocelyn walked through the door of his pub, he'd felt an instant attraction, quickly replaced with the need to offer her his protection.

He kenned the optics of it all. Especially now that she was under his employment. It could be misconstrued as him taking advantage of her. Something he would never do. His friends kenned that, but did everyone else?

"Have ye asked her to join us? Seeing how she and Lizzie got on at dinner, I think Lizzie would enjoy her being there. And only heaven kens what they are discussing now," he said with mirth, holding up his hand to inspect his perfectly manicured nails.

"I havena, though I was happy to see them getting along so well. 'Twas my hope. Jocelyn is hiding something. Maybe she'll talk about whate'er 'tis with Lizzie. But if no', that's what I expect ye to find out."

Malcolm blew out smoke and nodded. "I will do what I can. But have ye thought of the ramifications?"

He kenned this question would be coming sooner or later. It still didn't make him feel any better. "I am sure she will be upset if she finds out. 'Tis why I expect ye to keep mum on the matter."

"Or," Malcolm drawled, "Ye could gain her trust and wait for her to confide in ye."

"I could," Gunn admitted, "But I fear I've no patience to wait for the time."

With a curt nod, Malcolm straightened. "If ye dinna mind Lizzie staying here at the inn, I'll leave in the morn for Rochester."

>>><<<

"Did ye break your fast already?" Gunn asked from the doorway.

Jocelyn closed the ledger she had just finished reviewing. She woke up early this morning, wanting to get a head start on the books, but she did stop by the kitchen for a slice of toast and tea before beginning.

"You needn't worry. I ate this morn."

Smiling, he stepped inside. "I am glad to hear it. Have ye found more instances of unaccounted transactions?"

She nodded. "Unfortunately, yes." She handed him the list she was keeping.

He read through it, brows drawing down. She could understand why. The amounts were of substantial sums.

"I am sorry to be the bearer of bad news."

"Nay. Dinna apologize for that. 'Tis exactly what I wanted ye to identify. And identify ye have." He sighed, handing her the parchment. "Are ye almost through?"

Twisting her mouth, she dipped her head from side to side. "I'm more than three-quarters of the way done. But I still have a few to review. I hope to be done tonight."

"I do hope ye dinna plan to work the whole day and night, Jocelyn. Ye have plenty of time."

It was kind of him to say so. She wanted to make sure she was making herself useful. Dallying about and taking her time didn't seem like she was being helpful.

He narrowed his eyes. "Ye're going to work through the afternoon, are ye no'?"

The man could read minds. Or at least he could read her mind.

He shook his head, a wayward tendril of dark hair falling over his forehead. "No' today. Ye willna be doing such a thing." He planted his hands on his hips and looked around the small space. "Ye dinna get nearly enough light in here. Ye need a space that allows more sun. I'm going to move your desk."

She jumped up. "You do not need to do that. Honestly. These accommodations are perfectly fine. I am thankful for them."

"I willna take nay for an answer. But it may be the morrow before I can make the switch." He pulled a watch from his jacket pocket and checked the time. I will be back in two hours. At which time we will go for a walk."

It wasn't a question, or an offer. It was stated as fact.

He crossed his arms as he looked at her, daring her to challenge him. Truth be told, she liked the idea. It would give her another chance to learn more about him. To see the softer side of him when he let down his guard.

She dipped her head and pressed her lips together to hide her smile. When she was sure she could keep a straight face, she met his gaze. "That would be nice, thank you."

"I am glad ye agree. I will see ye then." He spun on his heel and left the room, leaving Jocelyn wondering what she was getting herself into.

She hadn't spent a large amount of time with the laird, but the time she had spent with him she enjoyed very much. Last night at dinner was a surprise. She didn't feel like his employee. Rather his partner. No, that wasn't the right designation either. She imagined last night would be what it felt like when two people were courting.

The smiles. The easy conversation. The sidelong glances that they hoped no one else noticed.

But just as soon as she thought such things, Victor popped into her mind, dampening her mood instantly.

She was still a married woman. She had no right getting involved with another man.

No matter how much care and concern he showed her. How handsome he was. How strong.

Lord above, Gunn could snap Victor like a twig with one hand. But that didn't matter.

She may have escaped him, but she was still bound to him.

And she loathed that fact. Mayhap luck would be on her side for once and he would just let her go. It would be nice if he would not bother looking for her.

But that was wishful thinking on her part, and she knew it.

No, she knew Victor. Too well.

He would never stop looking for her until he found her. His ego wouldn't allow him to lose her. He'd never be able to explain it away to his friends and he damn sure wouldn't tell them that she left of her own accord.

Because, really, with his ego he couldn't fathom how she would want to leave.

The bastard.

She was quite certain that he would rather see her dead than allow her the freedom she so longed for.

For the umpteenth time she hoped she'd run far enough north for him not to find her. Mayhap he was still running around southeast England questioning her old acquaintances to find out if they'd seen her. None had. Nor had they heard from her. Knowing it would be the first place he'd look, she made sure not to contact any of them.

"Hey," Lizzie called, drawing Jocelyn away from thoughts of Victor. "Are ye well? Ye look pale."

Jocelyn smiled. "I am fine. Thank you."

Lizzie didn't look convinced, but she didn't push any further. "Gunn told me I could find ye down here." She looked around the room and frowned. "Gads. Ye'd think he would have put ye someplace cheerier. This may as well be a dungeon."

Jocelyn laughed. "He came down earlier and alluded to the same.

Just not as colorfully as you. But he said he was going to move my desk to someplace sunnier."

"That's good. I would go mad being stuck down here."

Shrugging, she tucked a placeholder into the ledger she was reviewing and closed the cover. "I am just thankful for the job. It doesn't matter where I perform it."

Lizzie shook her head and clucked her tongue. "It does and ye should be honest with him."

"I am being honest. This room is fine. I wasn't expecting my own space." That was the truth. The room was fine. But she didn't want her own space and had hoped she would be working wherever Gunn was working. "Is there something that you needed?"

Lizzie looked confused. "Och, nay. I just wanted to see what ye were doing." She sat on a stack of boxes. "Malcolm left this morn, so I'm left to my own devices."

Her husband left? And left her here alone? That struck Jocelyn as odd. Why would he do such a thing?

Sensing her question, Lizzie waved her hand in the air in dismissal. "'Tis no' as bad as it sounds. Malcolm is an expert at information gathering. A skill he perfected in the war. He had an assignment, so he left to complete it. He should be back for the big gathering."

"What gathering?" Jocelyn wasn't aware of any meeting going on. Though why would she be?

Smiling slyly, Lizzie hopped off the boxes and approached the desk, leaning her palms on the edge. "The one I mentioned to ye yesterday. At Gunn's castle?"

Jocelyn closed her eyes and inwardly scolded herself. Of course. The get-together where all the friends and their wives and children would be in attendance. How could she have forgotten? Lizzie must think she was weak in the mind.

"Ah, yes," Jocelyn laughed to cover her embarrassment. "I remember now. I apologize, things have been hectic."

Lizzie furrowed her brows. "I hope Gunn is no' working ye too hard. Ye had a long journey to get here. Ye should be resting instead of working."

"Gunn has been most kind. I cannot complain about his treatment."

Lizzie straightened, seeming to accept Jocelyn's answer. "Ye are coming, arena ye?" she asked, focusing her attention back to the gathering.

She laughed nervously. "Oh, no, I don't think so. I wouldn't want to intrude, and besides, Gunn still hasn't asked me to go."

"Nonsense." She tucked a strand of dark hair behind her ear. "He just hasna gotten around to it yet. He will. He spoke of it last eve." Lizzie looked around the room and shuddered. "This room is making me feel enclosed." She came around the desk and pulled on Jocelyn's arm. "Let us go outside and get some fresh air."

Jocelyn bit her lip, indecisive. Gunn already said he would collect her for a walk. "I don't think I should. I've got lots left to do."

"Och, come on. I am sure it can wait."

"Gunn also said he would come get me this afternoon and we would go for a walk. I don't think he would be happy me taking a break before then."

Lizzie smiled. "Nonsense. I will let him ken I forced ye to join me outside."

Jocelyn wasn't convinced. She needed this position. It was the only way she could survive. She nibbled at her thumbnail as she pondered how to turn down Lizzie's offer and not offend her.

"Ye needna fash about Gunn. I promise." She clasped Jocelyn's hand and pulled her from the chair. "Besides, ye will find yourself ill if ye spend too much time in this space with these old musty crates. It canna be good for your health."

Laughing, Jocelyn shook her head. When she saw Gunn she would tell him that she would work late this eve to make up for the lost time.

CHAPTER EIGHT

G UNN WAS JUST finishing up wiping down the chairs and tables in the pub when the door burst open, and giggles filled the space.

He looked up, seeing a laughing Lizzie and a contrite Jocelyn. She looked at him nervously, worrying her lip with her teeth.

"Gunn. I've saved Jocelyn from that dreadful room ye've forced her into."

Quickly, Jocelyn spoke up. "She is jesting. I have no problem with my workspace. It contains all that I need."

Lizzie rolled her eyes at Jocelyn and turned to him. "She is being much too kind. It is dark and dank. What were ye thinking by sticking her in there?" She crossed her arms and pinned him with a severe glare.

"I have already informed Jocelyn that I will be moving her desk to some place more pleasant."

"I dinna ken how long ye have had her working where she is, but that is an idea ye should have had before now. Dinna ye think?"

Jocelyn stepped forward, looking guilty. "I apologize. I've waged no complaint over what you have provided, which has been more than accommodating. I will get back to work."

She spun on her heel and began to leave.

Lizzie glared at him, widening her eyes and gesturing to Jocelyn's retreating form. Like he was supposed to do something.

"Jocelyn," he called out.

She stopped, but didn't turn to face him. Just stood there, her head hanging before she spoke quietly. "I will work late this eve to make up for lost time. My apologies." She began to move forward again.

"Jocelyn, halt," he ordered, his voice sounding more stern than he meant. "I dinna care about your work time."

She spun, blue eyes clashing with his. "Lizzie is correct. 'Twas wrong of me to put ye in such a space. Ye should cease until I can move ye to a room up here."

"I was just going to take her outside so she could get some fresh air," Lizzie said, emphasizing the point as if he were daft.

"That's a wonderful idea."

"See, ye had naught to fash about."

He watched the whirl of emotions cross Jocelyn's face. The lass fashed too much. She was so concerned about not working hard enough. He'd be damned if he worked her to the bone. She still looked like she needed to hearty up.

"I will leave ye ladies to it, then. But Jocelyn?"

"Yes," she answered, her voice barely audible.

"Ye still owe me a walk," he said with a wink.

He could see the relief that sagged her shoulders. She dipped her head and then Lizzie was pulling her out the door.

He shook his head and pulled out a chair, sinking into it. The meeting he had with his solicitor earlier that day had gone much as he expected it to. There was little money to move around between his businesses and his estates. Gunn would need to make a decision soon.

Close, sell, or fund it from his other income sources, which right now, he had no other streams of revenue. Things were indeed looking dim for the Thistle & Pig and those he employed.

Looking around the pub, he thrummed his fingers along the polished wood of the tabletop. He'd furnished the space with the best tables. The most comfortable chairs. The finest liquor one could buy.

Once again, he thought about what had changed. Aye, Theodore was stealing from him. That was certain. And that explained his empty coffers, but it didn't explain why people stopped frequenting the pub. He had to get to the bottom of that. He had always had a good rapport with the townsfolk. He still seemed to when he crossed paths with them. Yet, they no longer walked through his doors.

Somehow, he believed Theodore was behind that as well, but why? What purpose could it serve him to kill his patronage? With the amount of coin he'd stolen, Gunn would think he would want to keep that up. He couldn't skim aught off the top when naught was coming in.

None of it made sense.

Mayhap after Malcolm returned with information about Jocelyn's past, he could look into what Theodore was up to.

The door opened and the subject of his thoughts walked in. "Good afternoon, Gunn."

Not ready to let Theodore ken he was on to his scheme, Gunn nodded in greeting. "What brings ye around?" It still wasn't his day to work. And surely he had better places to be.

"Was that Lady Kennedy out there with your new ward?"

He sighed, annoyed at the question. "Aye, and she isna my ward."

"Isna she?" he asked smartly, his eyes narrowing. "I see she is still here as I predicted."

Gunn ignored the jab. "She is under my employment now. What do ye need?" he asked again.

Theodore's eyes widened as he looked around the pub. "With what funds?"

Was he trying to figure out what Jocelyn was doing? Certainly he would never guess what her job entailed. And Gunn was not about to divulge that information.

"'Tis none of your concern." Gunn was growing tired of Theodore's presence. "Again, I ask is there something ye need?"

"Naught really. Just seeing how the pub was faring today."

Gunn pressed his lips into a thin line to keep from saying something he may regret later. Taking a deep breath, he blew it out slowly. "We have just opened, as ye ken. So no one yet."

He nodded. Gunn got the sense he was fishing for something. Information? He didn't ken, but whatever it was Gunn had no interest in offering him aught.

Theodore smiled. "Well," he bowed his head and tipped his hat. "I shall be on my way then."

With his arms crossed at his chest, Gunn watched him walk to the door.

Hand on the door, he paused. "Do let me ken if ye need me for aught," he called out nonchalantly and slipped through the door.

"Arsehole," Gunn muttered. He was up to something. He just didn't ken what. "Are ye set?" he asked Thomas.

The man nodded and Gunn dropped the cloth he'd been using to wipe everything down into a hamper behind the bar. "I'll be back later," he said and walked outside.

He was ready to walk with Jocelyn as he promised. He found her and Lizzie sitting on the bench outside the inn, watching the people pass by. He wished they would stop inside the pub for a drink, but that was a matter to think on later.

For now, he wanted to focus all his attention on Jocelyn.

"Ladies," he greeted, bowing deeply.

Jocelyn greeted him with a smile while Lizzie giggled.

He ignored her.

"Jocelyn, Lizzie. Would ye care to join me for a walk?"

Lizzie jumped up from the bench. "I actually have something that I need to do. I completely let it slip my mind. I'll leave ye two alone." When Jocelyn looked away from her, she waggled her eyes at Gunn.

The liar. She had naught to do, but he appreciated her lie.

They watched her walk into the inn.

"That was not so subtle," Jocelyn giggled.

Gunn couldn't help but laugh along with her. "No' at all." He offered his arm. "Would ye care for a stroll?"

For a moment she stared at his outstretched arm and he wondered if she would reject his offer. Finally, she smiled, and slipped her hand into the crook of his elbow.

"I would like that."

"I can show ye around our quaint little town."

They headed north, ambling along slowly as if neither of them had a care in the world. "I did some exploring on my own when I first arrived. It's quite nice."

"Thank ye. I enjoy the time I spend here."

She nodded. "I heard you have another estate, not too far from here."

He studied her profile as they continued down the street, and then turned right. He wasn't sure what he expected to see there. Something that would hint as to why she was here. And something darker.

What if she was here because of his failing business? Was it some grand scheme she was plotting? With his free hand he pinched the bridge of his nose. He didn't think that was the case. But considering his circumstances, he needed to be careful.

They passed the baker, and he noticed her deep inhale. The smile that just ticked up the corner of her mouth as she savored the delicious scents wafting out onto the street.

He had an idea. Tugging on her hand, he steered her to the door. "Let's see what sweet treat awaits us inside."

"Oh, I shouldn't."

Shifting so she could look at his face, he met her eyes. "Why no'?" He glanced over his shoulder at the display of pastries and tarts in the window. "I ken ye havena eaten aught since ye broke your fast this morn. And ye must admit," he took a deep breath, "Those scents are hard to resist. Dinna tell me ye doona like sugar."

She caught her lip in her teeth, trying to hide her smile, but it was too late. He'd seen it.

"See? I ken ye crave something from inside. Let's feed your hunger."

Cheeks flushed, Jocelyn finally acquiesced. But he couldn't tell if her blush was from excitement for the bakery or for the images his comments conjured up.

For him, all the heat he felt was due to having her in such close proximity to him.

And what he was craving couldn't be bought off the shelf in the bakery.

※※※

GUNN HELD OPEN the door of the bakery for Jocelyn to enter. Ducking under his outstretched arm, she walked into the welcoming place and was immediately enveloped with warmth and scents that soothed her soul.

"Sir Burnett," Liam, the baker greeted him cheerily.

"Liam. 'Tis nice to see ye. I see ye are making all the delights to tempt passersby again," Gunn stated.

The older man chuckled. "The misses and I have been busy." He looked at Jocelyn. "I dinna believe we've met, my lady. I'm Liam, the owner of this, if I do say so myself, fine establishment."

Jocelyn dipped into a curtsy. "It is very nice to meet you, Liam. Jocelyn. I'm staying at the inn."

"She is doing more than that. She is settling in to make Kincardine her home," Gunn stated.

Liam's face brightened. "Splendid. 'Tis a lovely place to settle down."

"I have found it very pleasant so far."

She chanced a sidelong glance at Gunn, but he was already looking at her and caught her gaze. She swore she saw him puff out his chest.

Was he trying to impress her? He needn't make grand gestures to do so. She daren't admit it, but she was quite enamored with him already. Him pontificating only made it that much harder to deny her feelings and hope that he felt just a smidge of what she did.

She noticed his clenched jaw and wondered what was on his mind. He cleared his throat, and tugged at his cravat, craning his neck.

"As we were passing by, we were sucked in by all the heavenly scents and had to come inside for a treat."

Liam smiled. "Whate'er ye fancy, ye just let me ken and I'll wrap it up for ye. How's business at the pub going?" he asked, his voice growing serious.

It seemed everyone in town knew the struggles Gunn was having with the pub, but yet, still no one came.

Jocelyn left them to speak about business, and browsed the cases filled with all the pastries she could imagine and then some. There were tarts of all flavors—berry, custard, onion. Petit fours in bright colors. Macarons with creamy filling. Croissants, currant muffins. Cranberry bread. The list of offerings went on and on.

She got the feeling that mayhap Liam's wife was French and the inspiration for many of the recipes. She couldn't be certain, but the store reminded her of a bakery she'd visited with her parents on a trip to Paris when she was young.

"See aught ye like?" Gunn said from behind her.

She hadn't heard him approach.

"So many things actually. How can one possibly choose?" She moved to another case that shelved beautifully decorated cakes of all flavors.

"He'll sell those by the slice if ye want just a taste. Or we can purchase the whole cake and ye can savor it for the week."

We can purchase the whole cake. Gunn made it seem as if this were a mutual venture. Like they were a couple strolling along and stopping for a treat.

Leaving the case of cakes, she walked over to a tiered stand that held pretty shaped shortbread. Everything looked divine, but she knew she couldn't afford aught in here. It was nice to dream of buying something, but it was out of the realm of possibility for her.

And she'd be damned to ask Gunn for a pay advance so she could purchase a treat.

"Actually, I am still quite full from my meal this morn."

Gunn lifted a brow in disbelief. He looked toward Liam, but the man was busying himself behind the counter. "I highly doubt the slice of toast ye had to break your fast is still in your belly, lass. Ye need to eat," he prodded, concern lacing his deep voice.

Instinctively, her palms went to her stomach, but she quickly dropped them as Gunn's eyes tracked the movement. He was right, of course, but he had no idea just how right he was.

Alas, it all came down to resources. And she was lacking in that department.

Apparently realizing that she wasn't going to give in and tell him what she wanted, Gunn approached the counter and told Liam they were ready to order.

Her eyes blew wide. No. She couldn't afford it. She hurried to his side. "Sir, I don't..."

Lifting his hand, he quieted her. "I find myself verra hungry. If ye dinna want aught, 'tis fine. I will order for myself."

She wanted to plead for him not to, because she knew what he was doing. Knew he'd figured out why she didn't want to order anything.

Minutes later they said their goodbyes to Liam and walked out of the bakery with Gunn carrying two large boxes of treats.

Her mouth had watered watching him pick out a variety of delectable desserts.

They headed back in the direction of the inn.

She leaned into him and bumped him in the side. "You didn't have to do that," she said quietly.

"I ken."

"Thank you."

"Ye're verra welcome. Now let's hurry back so we can enjoy these with tea."

Her eyes widened. "Surely you don't mean to eat all of these in one sitting."

Gunn barked out a laugh. "Nay, lass. But we can eat as many as we like, until our stomachs are bursting and we canna take another bite." He smiled, but then his expression grew serious. "Ye needna fash o'er purchasing such things. I would have ne'er brought ye inside to make ye pay for aught yourself. I want ye to eat well. To be happy."

She dipped her head, embarrassment heating her cheeks. He'd read her so well. Was she so bad at masking her feelings?

"Dinna be embarrassed, lass."

Apparently she was.

"We all have our paths. They are all different. Twisting and turning in their patterns. Some more difficult than others. When someone that has had an easier path offers ye a helping hand, dinna be afraid to accept it."

She bit her lip. His words cut her to the quick. It was as if he'd flayed her open and was reading all of her darkest secrets. He was far too observant.

Back at the inn, he ushered her into the dining room and sat her down at a table in the far corner, away from anyone that may happen to wander in. "I shall return shortly."

She nodded and watched him disappear through the door that led to the kitchens. No doubt he was ordering tea.

Returning a few minutes later, he was all smiles as he sat down across from her.

"Flora will be out shortly with tea." He passed her a linen napkin and she accepted it, unfolding it and laying it on her lap. Opening the boxes, he'd set on the table, he asked. "Which one would ye like to try first?"

"You should choose. You ordered them after all."

"For ye. I ordered them for ye. Since ye wouldna tell me what ye wanted, I got one of e'erything I thought ye might like."

Her eyes widened. "You did that for me?" The kind gesture had tears springing to her eyes. Quickly, she dabbed at the corners, hoping to stop them before they fell. What a fool he would think she was crying over desserts.

"Of course. Now, which one?"

Spotting a creme horn, she smiled. One of her favorite treats. It had been years since she'd had one. Pointing to it, she said, "That one."

"Ah, an excellent choice. Liam's wife, Annette, makes the best creme horns ye'll e'er taste." He plucked it out of the box and set it on a plate. "Here ye go."

"Thank you."

"Ye needna keep thanking me, lass. 'Tis my pleasure."

Heaven exploded in her mouth when she took a bite. She couldn't stop the groan of pleasure that escaped her lips.

Her eyes locked with Gunn's, his blue eyes darkening, as the tip of his tongue darted out to wet his lips.

Reaching out, he swept the pad of his thumb over the corner of her mouth, coming away with a small dollop of cream. Popping his thumb in his mouth, he sucked the cream from the tip.

Her skin heated. She'd never seen anything so wicked. Had never had such a thing happen to her before.

With a smile, he leaned in. "Ye had a wee bit of cream there." His voice was low, husky.

She opened her mouth to speak, but no words came out.

"So sweet," he said quietly. "Just like ye."

Had he really just said that? The treat in her hand suddenly forgotten, she focused her gaze on his full lips. What would it be like to feel them against hers?

She shook her head, trying to clear it. She was so desperate for affection that she was seeing things where they weren't.

But when her eyes clashed with Gunn's again, heavy emotion burned within his gaze. Was it passion?

"I've got your tea for ye," Flora announced beside the table.

Both of them quickly straightened, breaking eye contact, the connection lost. Fleeting.

Gunn cleared his throat. "Thank ye, Flora. Please leave it."

"Ye dinna want me to pour ye each a cup?"

"Nay. We are all set. Thank ye."

Jocelyn saw the way Flora's gaze slid over to her, brows arching high with a knowing smile on her lips. She curtsied and hurried from the room.

"I fear you have given her something to gossip about."

He chuckled. "Flora? Nay. That lass is loyal to a fault. He paused. "Hold on, what are ye referring to?" he asked, tilting his head innocently, but his eyes flared bright.

Did she dare tell him what she was thinking? That she wanted him to kiss her. That she wanted to get lost in the feeling of a passionate kiss by someone who cared?

She sighed. No. She didn't. "Did I tell you how much I appreciate you procuring all these desserts? I have no idea how I would ever eat them all, so I do hope you and the others will help eat them."

"Changing the subject are ye?" he said with a chuckle. "I'll allow it. For now," he smirked.

Taking another bite from the creme horn, she was careful to not let any of the creme escape. Because for certain, if he did that same move again, she would not be able to control her actions.

"May I ask ye a question?" His tone grew serious.

Nervously, her hand went to her stomach. Had he figured out she was with child? Nothing good could come of that. She thought she was doing a fair job of keeping the babe a secret. But as the months went along, it would be harder and harder to do so.

"Y-yes," she answered, her voice wavering.

"With the exception of last eve, when ye wore that lovely gold gown, why do ye always wear gray?"

Her shoulders sagged in relief. It wasn't about the babe. "Oh, I'm sorry to confess that it is the only color of gown I own. There's no real reason for it. It's just what I have." There was no way she was going to tell him that it was because it was the only color Victor would allow her to wear.

"Ye looked beautiful in gold last eve. I think I should like to see ye in vibrant colors that will complement ye."

She flushed. She couldn't afford to pay for sweet treats. She certainly couldn't afford to pay for a new wardrobe. It was on her list of things to acquire once she had secured lodging and settled. But until then, the gowns she arrived with would have to do.

"I think ye should take Lizzie to the modiste with ye and spend the day."

She waved her hand in front of her in dismissal. "I am fine. I've got work to do. The ledgers to continue reviewing. I am almost done." Panic rose in her throat. She didn't want the embarrassment of having to tell him she couldn't afford a handkerchief let alone a new gown.

"Jocelyn."

She stared into her tea, seeing the small bits of leaf floating in the steeped brew.

"Jocelyn," he called again. "Look at me."

He kept his voice gentle, but with enough seriousness in it to make her look up.

She met his eyes.

"I didn't offer that for it to cost ye aught. 'Tis my treat. Ye and Lizzie can make a day of it. The modiste can help ye choose colors to complement ye. Styles as well, whate'er ye need, she will help ye with."

He silenced her, putting up his hand. "I willna accept nay for an answer. I insist."

"What are ye insisting from the poor woman now, Gunn?" Lizzie said, breaking the tension that had begun to hang thick in the air.

"Lizzie, as always, ye have impeccable timing," Gunn quipped, standing to greet her.

She smiled wide. "Funny, Malcolm says the same thing. Och, are those desserts from Liam?" she asked excitedly.

"Yes, please sit and have one," Jocelyn offered. "Or three." She laughed.

Plucking a macaron out of the box, Lizzie looked at Gunn. "Well, must I ask a second time?" she prodded, rolling her eyes.

Jocelyn found herself really liking Lizzie. She loved her carefree spirit, and she wasn't afraid to speak directly.

"Ye are incorrigible. I dinna ken how Malcolm deals with ye."

"Splendidly," she countered, waggling her eyebrows.

"Well, since ye insist, I was just insisting that Jocelyn and ye should spend the day at the modiste. My treat."

"Och," Lizzie cooed, sitting forward. "'Twould be fun. I could use some new gowns. Especially since Malcolm has left me here. And with the upcoming trip to your estate. It makes no sense to go home, only to turn around and return." She turned to Jocelyn. "I dinna ken I've e'er seen him offer a treat such as that to anyone. Ye best take it while the offer is there." She sat back and nibbled on the macaron, a smile lifting the corners of her mouth.

She sighed. It appeared Gunn was set on his insistence, and Lizzie was all on board. "All right." She nodded and gave him a warm smile. "Thank you. Again."

Jocelyn wasn't used to such kind treatment, nor such generous offerings. Did Gunn make the same offers to every lass he met? Somehow, she didn't think so. And that realization had her dipping her head to hide a smile.

"Nay need to thank me, lass. 'Tis my pleasure." He pushed back from the table and stood up. "I shall leave ye two to plan your day." As he went to leave, he dipped his head and kissed her cheek.

Her mouth formed an 'O' in surprise and her hand fluttered to where his lips had just rested.

He snapped to his full height. Opened his mouth to say something and then snapped it shut before spinning on his heel and quickly walking out the door.

"Oh, my heavens," Lizzie exclaimed.

Jocelyn could feel the heat blooming on her cheeks.

"I told ye," Lizzie said. "There is attraction there."

CHAPTER NINE

If Gunn's friends could see him now, they would be hitting him with jabs and insulting him incessantly. He didn't ken what overcame him. It just felt natural that he kiss the lass goodbye. It wasn't aught he'd thought about doing beforehand.

It felt like a habit. And while he had to admit to himself, that was one habit he would gladly divulge in.

Groaning at what he'd just done, he scrubbed his face with his hands. On a positive note, she wasn't revolted at his actions. She seemed shocked but not disgusted.

That was a good sign, surely.

Thankfully, his friends hadn't arrived yet and weren't due to be here for several days. There was no one here to bear witness to what he'd done.

Save Lizzie.

Gunn groaned again. Hell, Lizzie would tell Gwen, Clarissa, and Willamina what he'd done within minutes of seeing them.

Mayhap he should feel shame for what he'd done. Or guilt. But he felt far from it. As a matter of fact, he wanted to march right back in there, sweep her up in his arms and kiss her properly. He wanted to see her lips swollen from his kisses.

Should he? The thought was tempting. If Lizzie weren't there, mayhap he would have. Though why he was allowing her presence to stop him he had no idea. From the looks of things, she would be well in favor of it.

He sighed, pushing his hands through his hair. Everything he'd done since Jocelyn arrived was against the norms of society. They were constantly alone. No chaperone in sight. Aye, Jocelyn kept saying she didn't need one, but to others watching them, they didn't ken that.

He tried to walk away, but an invisible force kept drawing him back. It was as if he was tethered to Jocelyn, and he couldn't be more than a certain distance away from her.

He was going mad. That was the only conclusion to be drawn from this situation. Was it so bad that he only wanted to make the lass smile? To see her eyes crinkle with happiness.

Happiness that he was the source of.

※

Jocelyn could barely contain her excitement as she and Lizzie made their way to the modiste. She had no right to be this happy. She'd been floating in the clouds since Gunn had kissed her.

She fought a giggle. She couldn't really call it a kiss. It was a quick peck and one-sided. And then Gunn disappeared before she could even react.

"What has ye smiling as if things canna get any better?" Lizzie asked as she looped their arms together.

"It's nothing. I'm just happy to be going to the modiste."

"'Tis fun, isna it?"

Jocelyn shrugged. "I believe it will be. I haven't been to one in quite some time."

Lizzie frowned, but the look was fleeting, and she quickly replaced it with a smile. "Ye will love the modiste here. Madame Gossard is wonderful. Not quite as good as the one I use at home, but nearly. Ye will love her."

"I feel guilty though."

"Whye'er for?"

"It's a big expense."

"Pfft. Gunn contacted Madame Gossard already and let her ken there shall be no limit." Lizzie clapped her hands. "We are going to get ye a whole new wardrobe."

Jocelyn smiled, but guilt consumed her. She'd seen the status of Gunn's finances and knew that he couldn't afford to extend her such a luxury. Not only that, all the money that would be spent would be a waste in the coming weeks when the babe started to grow. Mayhap she could request the modiste add some extra yards so she could wear them throughout her pregnancy.

"We're here," Lizzie said excitedly, practically pulling Jocelyn through the door.

A woman that looked to be about Jocelyn's age greeted them happily. She had rosy cheeks and kind eyes. Jocelyn liked her right away.

"Ladies, come in, come in." She waved her arms to hurry them inside. "Lady Kennedy, 'tis lovely to see ye again." She dropped into a curtsy. "And ye must be Lady Townsend. I'm happy to make your acquaintance."

"Please, just call me Jocelyn. I am not a lady."

"No' yet. She will be before we ken it, though," Lizzie said conspiratorially.

Madame Gossard's eyebrows shot up.

Jocelyn shook her head viciously. "She is jesting. I am not."

"'Tis no' my place to tell. Your secret is safe with me," she said with a wink.

"Why would you say such a thing?" she snapped at Lizzie when Madame Gossard left to gather some bolts of fabric for them to look at. "You have no idea of what you speak."

Hurt darkened Lizzie's eyes. "I am verra sorry. 'Twas just a jest. I meant no harm by it."

"It wasn't funny."

"I can see that ye didna think so. Forgive me?" She clasped Jocelyn's hands, swinging them to and fro, her lower lip stuck out in a pout.

She was impossible to stay mad at. No harm was done with her words. They were the only ones in the shop, so no one could overhear.

"Look," Jocelyn nodded in the direction of the counter. "Macarons. I bet they are from Liam, the baker. Let's have one while we wait."

There were several flavors on the platter. Jocelyn picked a pistachio one and as she expected, it was delicious as ever. Lizzie went for a vanilla macaron and smiled when she took a bite.

"Definitely one of Liam's." She licked her lips and dropped into a nearby chair. "Ye might as well sit. We'll have lots of fabrics to go through when Madame Gossard returns."

But as soon as Jocelyn sat, her stomach lurched. She quickly stood, clutching her middle.

Springing into action, Lizzie jumped up. "Ye look like ye are going to be ill."

"I need—" Unable to finish the sentence because she would lose the contents of her stomach right then and there, she rushed to the side door and ran outside. She just made it to a bush before vomiting.

"Are ye feeling unwell, Jocelyn?" Lizzie asked, her voice filled with concern. "Mayhap we should return to the inn and reschedule."

Once she her stomach was empty, Jocelyn felt much better. Wiping her mouth with the handkerchief Lizzie offered, she flattened her palm on her belly. The babe was letting him or herself be known. And that worried her more than anything.

"No. I am fine now."

"Ye didna look fine, but now your color appears to be coming back. Are ye sure? We can return at another time."

Jocelyn shook her head. "I am fine, truly."

Lizzie gave her the side-eye, but didn't push any further. "Well, then, let's go inside and see what fabrics and colors have been chosen for ye." She spun back to look at Jocelyn. "But, if at any point ye feel ill, let me ken. Madame Gossard will be more than happy to change our appointment."

Jocelyn gave Lizzie what she hoped looked like an encouraging smile. "There will not be any need for that. Thank you for your concern, though. It's very kind of you."

Back inside, they sat at a long table where Madame Gossard had laid out several bolts of fabric of varying textures and colors.

"Och, ye must use this gold fabric, Jocelyn. It suited ye so well the other night."

"That is a lovely shade. I just got it in from France," the modiste added. "Do ye ken what kind of styles ye are looking for?"

Jocelyn worried her lip. She hadn't the faintest idea. All her gowns followed the same style, and she was not on top of what the latest fashions were. "I would love to have your input on that, Madame Gossard. As the dressmaker, you must have great insight into which styles would fit me best." She hoped the way she asked didn't let either the modiste or Lizzie know that she was uncertain.

"Well, now that ye ask, I do. I had pictures flood my mind as soon as ye walked in the door. If ye trust me, I'd love to surprise ye."

She slid her gaze to Lizzie, quietly seeking her thoughts. The woman nodded her head enthusiastically.

"I would like that very much, Madame."

Madame Gossard clapped her hands in excitement. "Wonderful!" She gestured for her to come near. "Let's get ye measured, and then we can choose colors. And ye can let me ken what items ye need."

Oh, that was something she hadn't thought about. What items did she need? Considering her wardrobe consisted of two gowns, and some undergarments, she supposed she would need a lot. But the cost would be high. She didn't want Gunn to think she was taking advantage of his generosity.

"She needs a whole wardrobe, Madame."

Jocelyn gasped. "Lizzie!" Embarrassed, she felt her cheeks flush.

Lizzie shrugged. "'Tis naught to be embarrassed about. Gunn told me right before we left that he wanted me to ensure that ye didna hold back and ordered a full wardrobe."

"How verra kind of him," Madame chimed in. "He must care for ye aplenty."

"Well, I do not know about that, but he has been very kind since my arrival." She stepped onto the raised dais, and madame approached, measuring tape in her hand. As Lizzie lost herself in going through the fabrics on the table, Jocelyn took advantage of her distraction to speak quietly with madame.

"May I ask ye a private favor?" she whispered.

Madame paused, her hands mid-air as she was measuring her arm-length. "Of course. What can I help ye with?"

"Is it possible to, er," oh, how could she ask this delicately? Deciding that there wasn't a way other than to just come out and say it, she continued. "Would it be possible for you to make the gowns and items a size or two larger than needed?

Madame's brows drew together as she contemplated her question. Jocelyn could practically see the wheels turning as she pondered, sure she was trying to put two and two together to figure out the reason why she would ask such a thing.

"I suppose I could if that is what ye want, but ye wouldna want a poor-fitting gown, would ye? It wouldn't put forth the best appearance. For ye or the laird."

She didn't want to make people think that Gunn wasn't treating her well by putting her in ill-fitting gowns. "Mayhap, whichever styles ye choose cannot be form-fitting around the middle, and will fall loosely?"

Madame gasped, her eyes rounding before she glanced at Lizzie and then quickly back to her, nodding her head. "I believe I ken what ye are saying. Have no fear, your secret is safe with me."

Jocelyn nibbled at the nail bed of her thumb nervously. What had she done? She'd told a stranger that she was expecting. She wanted to cry.

Madame placed a light hand on her arm. "Truly. Ye wouldna believe the things I hear when people visit my shop." She giggled. "I have gossip on nearly every person that I've made an item for. Believe me when I tell ye, your secret will never pass my lips."

"Thank you," Jocelyn whispered, relief flooding through her.

"I will do what I can to make ye fashionable items that ye can grow into. How's that?"

Jocelyn nodded. "I appreciate that."

"Now, let's finish these measurements and get to the fun part. Choosing your colors." She smiled warmly and went back to work.

Daring a look at Lizzie, Jocelyn was happy to see that she wasn't paying any attention to them.

It wouldn't be long before signs of the babe would be visible. She had to brace herself for the time when she would have to explain it to Gunn.

A conversation she wasn't looking forward to.

CHAPTER TEN

GUNN HEARD THE women approach before he actually saw them. Loud giggles filled the air. He couldn't help but smile. He was right when he thought Lizzie would do Jocelyn good.

He hadn't seen Jocelyn since his impromptu kiss on the cheek the night before. He still couldn't believe what had overcome him. For whatever reason, it had just seemed like the natural thing to do.

Did he regret it? Not one wee bit.

The door opened, and the two women swept inside, smelling like fresh air and the perfume that he could only assume the modiste used in her shop.

Jocelyn stopped short when she saw him, biting her lip nervously, as she shifted from foot to foot.

Lizzie looked between them and got that glint in her eye that Gunn had begun to realize was trouble. "I will leave ye two alone. There is something I must attend to after being away all afternoon." Faster than he'd ever seen her move before, she disappeared, leaving just him and Jocelyn in the inn reception area.

"Did ye have a fun afternoon at the modiste?" he asked, not wanting to bring up the awkwardness of the night before.

"Very much so. Once again, I must say thank you," she said shyly. "I know you do not have the funds for such an extravagant outing and—"

Gunn held his hand up, stopping her midsentence. "Dinna mention it. Ye deserve it. Ye've done much for me since ye've arrived."

Time seemed to stand still, the air thick with tension. He would in no way admit to her that he'd taken the last of his available funds to fund her afternoon outing. He had until the end of the month, the middle of next month at the very latest, to turn things around. After that? Well, he would accept defeat and sell. As much as it pained him to do so.

"Are ye hungry?"

"No," she shook her head emphatically. "We actually had snacks at the modiste."

"Tea then?"

He hadn't the slightest idea why he always offered the lass tea. Aye, it was what she drank, but usually he would leave the tea offers to Flora. But it was as if he needed a reason for her not to leave his side. He took a tentative step toward her.

Paused.

Waited to see if she backed away from him.

To his surprise, she took a step forward.

His brows lifted, and he caught his lip between his teeth.

She looked beautiful this afternoon, a healthy glow that he was glad to see warmed her cheeks. Her bruises were all but gone. Unless ye kenned they were there, ye wouldn't ken.

This time, they both took a step at the same time, and then another, until they were standing so close, he could feel the heat emanating off her body. Her drab gray gown did naught to dwindle her attractiveness.

Taking a dare, he reached out, resting his hands on her hips. He waited a beat. Waited to see if she would push him away. Turn tail and run.

She did none of those things.

Instead, she surprised him and wrapped her hands around his biceps, looking up into his eyes. Her irises the color of the sea, emotion roiling within their depths and he wondered if he was dreaming.

"About last night," he whispered.

Jocelyn shook her head. "Don't."

"Dinna what?"

"Don't apologize. If that's what you were going to do, please don't. I'm not sorry. Surprised? Yes, verra much so. But I didn't mind."

His tongue darted out, wetting his lips as her teeth worried her bottom lip, making it plump. Juicy. He wanted to suck it into his mouth. Taste her. Drink her in.

"I want to kiss ye," he murmured.

She lifted her face to his, meeting his eyes. "What are you waiting for then?"

His body roared to life at the invitation. He pulled her closer, so her body was flush with his. Watching the emotions play on her face for a few long moments, before he finally brought his head down and captured her mouth with his.

With a sigh, she melted into him, her palms sliding up to his shoulders.

He dropped his hands to her buttocks, grinding his hips into her as his tongue sought entry. When she opened her mouth on a gasp, his tongue joined hers, dancing wickedly together to a tune as old as the stars.

She tasted of mint, and he couldn't get enough. When they broke apart for air, they both were breathing heavily, chests heaving. Her cheeks were flushed, her blue eyes almost the color of midnight now.

Bringing her hands forward, she grasped the lapels of his jacket, tugging him down to her once again. This time, it was she who initiated the joining of their mouths.

Damn. This woman was perfect. Not scared to go after what she wanted. He kenned she could feel his hardened length against her stomach and even that didn't have her stopping.

Christ. He scooped her up into his arms and pushed through the door that would lead him down the hall to his room. Once inside, he kicked the door shut, reaching back to engage the lock.

Continuing the kiss, he walked to the bed and laid her gently down.

She propped herself up on her elbows, looking at him with a wicked glint in her eyes as she licked her lips.

Hell's teeth, the lass was insatiable. He tugged at his cravat, untying it. "Anytime ye want me to stop, ye say the word, lass."

She shook her head, biting the tip of her finger. "I won't." She came forward, grabbing the ends of his cravat and pulled him down to her, feathered kisses on his cheeks, before whispering in his ear, "I want this."

His eyes rounded. "What did that modiste do to ye, lass?" he chuckled.

She laughed. "Is it wrong that I've decided to stop fighting the war that has been raging inside of me since I first saw you?"

"Nay," he said breathlessly, as she kissed his chest, her breath tickling the smattering of hair.

She stood up, wrapping her arms around his neck. "Will you think less of me if I do?"

"Nay." It was as if she'd stolen all thought from his brain and he couldn't come up with more than one-word answers. Snapping out of it, realizing the levity of their current situation, he needed to ensure she was certain. No matter how much he wanted her, he wasn't about to ruin her. "Ye need to be sure ye want this. I've wanted ye in my arms since the verra moment ye walked into my pub."

She smiled. "I'm glad it was your pub I walked into."

"As am I. But I mean it. I willna be the cause of your downfall. Or ruin."

"You needn't worry about such things. I'm a grown woman, able to make my own decisions about what I want." She gave him a quick kiss on the lips. "And right now, I want you. If you'll have me."

He groaned, his head craning back. "Seriously, lass, ye must ask?"

He grasped her hand and flattened her palm against his cock, hard and straining for release.

Eyes wide, she smiled. "I have something to confess. I don't think it would be right to continue without you knowing."

He nuzzled her neck. "Ye can tell me aught and it willna sway me from my wants and thoughts right now."

Suddenly, she looked nervous. He felt her hands ball into fists behind him and her face take on a pained look.

"I'm married."

>>><<<

HAD SHE REALLY just announced that right as they were getting ready to lay together? Yes, she had. She felt that it was necessary. She wanted him to know exactly what he was getting into with her before diving in headfirst. Deceit wasn't in her blood, and she couldn't do that to him.

"Come again?" he asked in disbelief, pulling away from her.

Immediately, she missed the heat of his body.

She sighed and sank down onto the soft mattress, her fists bunching the fabric of the gray duvet. "I am married. I'm so sorry. I'm not with my husband. I, he's not a nice man."

His eyes narrowed. He pushed his hands through his hair, scrubbing his face with his palms. "How long?" he asked, his voice clipped.

"How long for what?"

He let out a long breath and backed away from the bed. Walking over to the sideboard, he poured himself a glass of what she assumed was whisky. "Have ye been married?"

"Six years," she answered quietly.

"Jesus." He pinched the bridge of his nose and shook his head. "Does he ken ye are here? Ye shouldna be here."

"No! I made sure I ran to a place he wouldn't expect. I don't want him to find me."

Confusion drew his brows down, as he frowned. "I, all right." He sat in a chair in front of the small fireplace, his head in his hands. "I cannot be so close to you right now."

She swallowed down the hurt that his words caused, but she understood. And it just confirmed that she'd done the right thing when she did. "I understand. I've been dishonest."

"Nay. I dinna believe ye have. Ye just havena been forthright."

"That either."

"Tell me," he ground out.

She could tell he was angry. And that he was barely containing it. Knowing she was the cause of his anger made her upset. But she could understand why. She had just confessed to something that held a huge weight.

"I was married six years ago. Not my choice, really. It was arranged by my parents. Victor, my husband, was very charming in the beginning, until we were married, then it all changed. He was not a nice man. Cruel."

"Your bruises," he said quietly. "He beat ye?"

It was embarrassing to admit. But she needed to tell him the truth. She didn't love Victor. Hadn't in a very long time, if ever.

"He did. Often. With his fists and his feet. It didn't matter what I did. It angered him. Everything I did was wrong. Or not good enough. Or not fast enough. There was always a reason."

"The bastard. What of your parents? Did they ken?"

She shrugged, wringing her hands together. "Maybe, but they passed shortly after we married."

"I'm sorry, lass. Were ye close?"

She pressed her lips together, wondering how she could put their relationship into words. "Not overly, but we loved each other very much, if that makes sense. I have great memories from my childhood, but they weren't very emotional."

"Did they see how ye were being mistreated?"

She shook her head. "No. After I was married, Victor made sure that he was my focus. There were no trips to visit them. I could no longer speak to my friends. He got very angry when I did, and I found it easier to just let them go instead of angering him about it."

"This last beating. It had to have been bad for ye to still have the bruises after journeying all this way."

Thinking back to that night, she squeezed her eyes shut. The anger blazing in Victor's eyes as he reigned down punch after punch. She shielded her stomach, not wanting any harm to come to the babe. When he'd finally exhausted himself, he'd shut himself in his study.

She nodded. Memories flooded her and she fought back tears. She wouldn't cry in front of Gunn. She didn't want his pity.

"I had been planning to leave for some time before that. But that night, it was just so bad. I couldn't wait any longer."

Gunn pushed off from the chair and came to sit next to her on the bed.

She welcomed his closeness.

"Ye made the trip alone?"

"Yes, with money I had stashed away over time." She laughed nervously. "Money, that as you know, ran out when I got here."

"Ye are a strong woman."

"I don't know about that. I stayed for six years."

"But ye kenned to leave before it was too late."

She had to tell him the rest. But the words hung heavy in her throat, cutting off her air. But she was all about honesty on this night. If they wanted to pursue a relationship, lord, is this what they were doing? She didn't even know. One thing she did know was that if there was any chance for them, any at all, she needed to speak the truth. All of it. As ugly as it may be.

Even if it meant that he put her out on the street as he soon as he learned her secret. It was the only way she would be able to live with herself.

She was tired of hiding.

"There is one more thing. And it was the catalyst for me running that night and why I couldn't wait any longer."

Gunn studied her face as if he was trying to read what it was through her expression. He clasped her hand in his, his thumb stroking over her skin in a gesture that offered her comfort.

"Whate'er 'tis, I'm here. Ye are the strongest woman I have e'er kenned. To do what ye did, ye are amazing."

She bit her lip, worried that he would want to take that back when he heard what she had to say.

He must have sensed that she was holding back. He squeezed her hand. "I'm no' going anywhere, lass. Well, I may go down to Rochester and kill your husband, but other than that, I'm no' going anywhere."

She smiled, knowing he was trying to lighten the mood. Though she had no doubt that he could easily handle Victor.

She inhaled a shuddering breath and let it out slowly. Gunn was looking at her intently, urging her on.

Finally, she met his eyes, and blurted, "I'm with child."

CHAPTER ELEVEN

Gunn felt like he'd just been sucker punched. "Pardon?" he ground out.

Jocelyn brought her hands up to shield her face. "I'm pregnant. I'm sorry. I should have told you sooner. It's why I finally ran." She stood stiffly. "I will go."

He reached out for her arm as she passed. "Jocelyn. Lass." The look she gave him broke his heart. Clearly, she had been dealing with so much more than she'd let on. "Ye dinna have to go."

Her eyes clashed with his, shiny with unshed tears. He didn't think she should be alone. Her emotions were at a tipping point, and he thought she could use some encouragement, not a shunning.

Which he would never do in the first place.

Leading her over to the chairs by the fireplace, he urged her to sit. Then he went and grabbed some wine. Pouring her a glass, he handed it to her and took a seat across from her.

"Ye needna fear my reaction. I would be lying if I said I wasna taken aback. 'Twas just a shock, is all."

She moved the glass around in circles, causing the liquid inside to create a slight vortex.

"Are you going to end my employment?" she asked quietly, not meeting his eyes.

"Of course no'," he spat. "Though I believe we have stepped past that, but there are other priority items we must discuss." If she hadn't realized it before, he didn't want her as an employee. Hell, he'd keep her in his bed every night for eternity and would love every minute of it. If she wanted to help him, then fine.

But as partners.

He pinched the bridge of his nose. Shite. This situation presented a myriad of problems.

"Tell me e'erything."

Her head snapped up. "I have."

"Nay. Your history. I want to ken it all. Parents. Husband." He gestured to her still flat belly. "The bairn."

Pressing her lips together, she folded her hands on her lap, before quickly unfolding them to wring them together. "How much time do you have?" she asked with a nervous laugh.

He kenned she was trying to lighten the mood, and realized he needed to school his face into a more neutral look. He wasn't angry with her. But that louse that she was married to? Aye. He would be dealing with him.

"All the time ye need," he said gently, offering what he hoped was an encouraging smile.

"When I was younger, and it was time to be introduced into society, I begrudged the whole thought of it. I didn't want to spend my nights being looked over like a prized pony. Victor, my husband, appeared out of nowhere. He was handsome enough. But especially charming. He showed interest and I saw him as my salvation to save me from the prancing required in society. It was easier to court him from the beginning. He won over my parents, convincing them that we were the perfect match, and got their blessing quickly. The three of them came to an agreement and after that there was no way for me not to marry Victor.

"My friends were happy but jealous. Victor was the bachelor of the season." She sighed, sad eyes meeting his. "But it was all a lie. He didn't care for me, just my healthy dowry. He was cruel. Both in speech and in body. I could do naught right."

Gunn's fists clenched. He understood where this was going. And he didn't like one bit of it. Men who beat their wives were the scourge of the earth. They didn't deserve to be called men.

"Of course," she continued. "He didn't show any of those traits until after we married, and we returned from holiday. Quickly, he moved us away from my family and friends, to Rochester."

He wanted to cut in so many times as she talked. Wanted to pull her into his arms and offer her comfort. Something her arsehole of a husband never did. He wanted to kiss away all her fears. Her worries.

Every inch of skin that was ever marred with a bruise.

"After we were in Rochester, I got to see the real Victor. The cruel man hiding behind a facade of a caring face. He disliked me keeping in contact with my friends, and soon I found it easier to let them go then withstand the beating I would get whenever I met up with them. My parents were next." She let out a shuddering breath. "It had been quite some time since I'd spoken with them when I got word of their passing." A tear slipped from her eye, trailing down her cheek and she swept at it. Offering her a handkerchief, she gave him a sad smile and dabbed at her eyes.

"I'm sorry, lass." His parents had been gone for a long time. But he felt it was different for women. The bond they had with their mothers was special. For her husband to rip that support system away from her was cruel.

"Before I knew it, he'd sold their house and all their belongings."

Gunn's ire grew. The man was truly a piece of shite.

The fire crackled, a loud pop sending sparks through the air, causing Jocelyn to jump.

Taking a small sip of wine, she shakily set the glass back down on the small rectangular table set beside the chair. Her fingers traced the stack of books the table held.

"Were ye able to return before the purchasers took ownership?" he asked, hoping that the louse at least allowed her that.

"Yes, but only for a few short moments. I couldn't take anything because he'd sold everything inside. But in a short respite when he was engrossed in conversation with the buyer, I managed to grab my mother's diary and hide it within my reticule." She looked at him sadly. "It's the only thing I have left of either of my parents."

"I canna imagine how hard that must have been for ye. How hard it still is."

"Very. But I still have my mother's writings. Other than the few items of clothing I left with, I made sure I had that. Her words are comforting."

A faint smile tipped the corners of her mouth at the memory of her mother.

"I'm glad ye still have those. And that they offer ye comfort."

"Thank you. You know that he beat me. I thank you for offering me grace when I arrived and not pushing me for details. I had been saving money for quite some time. A pence here. A pence there. My leaving was always going to happen. I just didn't know when. When my courses were late, I knew the time had come. I left that night."

"Ye are a verra strong woman, Jocelyn. Dinna let anyone e'er tell ye otherwise."

She twirled the corners of his handkerchief into little corkscrews. Unfurled them. Twisted them again. "I'm not sure I believe that," she confessed.

"How can ye no'? Look how far ye traveled. Alone. When 'tis no' safe."

"I needed to get as far away as possible. My friends are south of Rochester. I knew that's where he would look first, so I went north. My plan was always to escape to Scotland. And here I am."

He smiled. "Here ye are indeed."

Brows drawing down, she met his eyes. "I understand if you want to put me out. I would expect nothing less for my deception."

"Lass," he dropped to his knees in front of her, fingers on her chin to draw her gaze. "If ye think I would do that, ye surely dinna ken me at all." He tucked a loose strand of hair behind her ear. "My feelings are still true. Does this change our trajectory? Aye. But I will help ye with this. We will get through this together."

"You don't have to do that. I will find a way."

"I believe ye have misunderstood me. I am no' letting ye go, Jocelyn Townsend. I have resources at my disposal. Friends that will help. Their wives who will welcome ye gladly into their circle. Dinna fash."

"Your kindness," she paused. "I don't know what to say."

"Answer me something? Truthfully. No matter if ye think I will be hurt by your answer, I want the truth. Understood?"

She nodded, tucking the corner of her lip behind her teeth.

"Did ye ever love your husband?"

THE QUESTION TOOK Jocelyn off guard. Though it shouldn't have. It was only normal for Gunn to inquire about her feelings regarding Victor.

She sighed heavily and shook her head. "At one point, I thought I did. When we were courting. But, I haven't for years. Whenever I questioned it, I'd been told it wasn't uncommon for spouses not to love each other. My parents had a loving relationship, but Victor always called them an anomaly. But no, I don't love him. I don't think I ever really did."

The feelings she had at the beginning of their courtship, she now understood them to be an infatuation. An escape. How ironic was it that she saw Victor as an escape from her familial duties to find a reputable husband only to find out that it was he that she would need to escape from in the end?

Gunn smiled and sat back in his chair. "'Tis settled then."

Confused, she looked at him. "What is?"

"We will find a way to deal with all of this. Together." His tone grew serious. "Unless that is no' what ye want. In which case, we will do whate'er ye feel is best for ye."

Was Gunn offering her what she thought he was? He wasn't going to kick her out onto the street. He had every right to, but instead he was supporting her. The feeling was so foreign to her.

"This is what I want," she said quietly. "When I arrived it wasn't what I expected or even thought about, but it is. I thank you for giving me a choice. Something that was stolen from me long ago."

"Lass, ye will always have a choice with me. Remember that."

She nodded, she could never show him how much she appreciated his support. She would try, but she feared it would never be enough.

"First thing, I need to call Malcolm back."

"I thought he had work."

"He did, but it was at my order."

Confused, she waited to see if he would expand on his answer.

Sheepishly, he met her eyes. "I sent him to Rochester."

"Pardon? Why would you have done such a thing?"

"You showed up here, out of the blue, clearly beaten, with hardly any belongings, looking for a place to live and work. Without ye being forthcoming of your circumstances, which I dinna place any blame on ye," he quickly added. "But with that, I needed to see what your background was."

She contemplated his words. They made sense. Clearly he would have been suspicious. She would have been the same if the roles were reversed. "That's understandable, considering how I arrived. You are very kind to offer me assistance."

"Have ye eaten aught hearty today? Ye mentioned snacks at the modiste. But ye need food. Good, healthy sustenance for the bairn." He stood, grasped her hand and pulled her up. "Let's go see what Cook has for ye."

She worried her lip, unsure if he understood everything he could be getting himself into.

Sensing her hesitation, he turned her to face him. "What is wrong?"

She'd already laid out her life story before him. The good, the bad. The horrible. She might as well be forthright with any questions she had going forward.

"What are we doing?" She pointed her index finger back and forth between them. "What is this?"

"Well," he drawled, drawing her close with his arms wrapped around her waist. "I guess ye could call it courting. I havena any experience in that, but that is the first step, am I correct?"

"Are you suggesting what I think you are?" she whispered, her heart skipping a beat. But there were so many hurdles for them to jump through to get to any secure future she didn't dare hope for a relationship between the two of them.

"If ye are thinking marriage, then aye." He pulled her in for a hug, and she took comfort in his warm embrace, her head resting on his chest. She could feel his warmth. Feel the thump of his heart. His lips in her hair. She closed her eyes and savored the moment.

"But how? And do you know what that means?" She pushed back so she could meet his eyes. "What you are burdening yourself with?"

"We will figure out the semantics in dealing with Victor. There's divorce, and whilst no' common, 'tis possible. Again, I have friends that have a lot of pull when it comes to matters such as these. They hold sway and if we canna get Victor to acquiesce and agree to a divorce, we will force him to."

She widened her eyes. "I do not want to cause any trouble."

"Lass," he chuckled. "When will ye realize ye are worth it?"

Was she? She'd spent years listening to her worth was only in the monetary value she brought to the marriage.

"I can sense that ye are trying to justify that in your mind. Dinna do that to yourself. Dinna let him win when ye've finally found your freedom."

She laid her head on his chest once again. Gunn's hands gently ran up and down her back, soothing her nerves. "And the babe?" she asked quietly.

"I have always wanted children."

It was a statement. Said with conviction. No waver in his voice.

"That is a lot to accept. A child that is not yours. You would raise it as your own?"

"'Tis no' the bairn's fault how he or she came to be in the world. What matters is they have two loving parents to raise them and shower them with affection."

"I." She was at a loss for words. Gunn was almost too good to be true. How had she gotten so lucky? Out of all the pubs she could have entered, she went into the one that would prove to be her future.

"Say naught, lass. 'Tis a lot to digest. But I promise ye, all will work out in the end. Now, let's go get ye something to eat. Ye're eating for two, after all."

She let Gunn take her hand and lead her to the kitchen.

Lizzie was in the drawing room as they passed. She jumped up from her chair where she'd been playing solitaire. "Where have ye two been?" she asked, her hands on her hips before her eyes darted from one to the other, narrowing as her suspicion grew.

Gunn turned to Jocelyn. "Mayhap ye and Lizzie have much to discuss. How about ye do that o'er food?" He smiled. "I shall contact Malcolm."

"Why do ye need Malcolm?"

But Gunn just dipped his head and placed a soft, lingering kiss on Jocelyn's cheek. "Eat. And I mean it." Then he disappeared down the hall.

"What is going on?" Lizzie demanded. "Something has happened."

Jocelyn giggled. "I have lots to tell you. Much has happened since we arrived home."

Over tea, dried meat, cheese, and fruit, Jocelyn explained all that had transpired since they'd arrived home from the modiste. With eyes wide, Lizzie listened intently, sometimes gasping, other times clapping her hands in delight.

"Ye just wait. The ladies are going to love this story. And a bairn!" She clapped again. "Happy times indeed."

"You don't think it is too much? For Gunn, I mean."

"Nay. Gunn is strong. Also, determined. When he says he's going to do something, he will fight to the teeth to get it done."

Jocelyn sighed in relief. With a groan, she pushed her plate away. "I cannot eat another bite."

"Ye ken Gunn is going to be constantly feeding ye from here on out? He'll want to ensure ye have the healthiest bairn."

"He is very kind. I only hope I can keep it all down." She rubbed her stomach. "This meal seems fine, but the snacks at Madame Gossard's did not settle well."

"Mayhap they were too rich for your stomach. When e'eryone arrives, we'll have to discuss stomach remedies with Gwen, Clarissa, and Willamina. They'll surely have some suggestions with dealing with that. They've all had at least one bairn or one on the way." She sipped her tea and suddenly set her cup down with a clank. "Your bairn will grow up with the others. How exciting is that?"

Jocelyn wasn't sure. She wasn't even sure if the others would accept her. What if they thought she was taking advantage of Gunn? It was something she didn't want to think about right now.

Setting her napkin on the table, she pushed her chair back. "It has been a long day. I think I should get some rest."

Thanking Cook for the meal, she made her way upstairs to her room. At the top of the stairs, a man waited near her door. He was vaguely familiar. Nervously, she looked around. No one else was there.

The man approached, greeting her with a smile that didn't quite reach his eyes.

"Jocelyn?" he asked.

Immediately, she didn't trust him. When she turned to go back downstairs, he rushed forward and grabbed her roughly by the arm. Putting a finger to her lips, he willed her to be silent.

"I would like a few words before you retire for the eve."

The hairs on her arms stood up. She remembered where she'd seen him before. It was Gunn's business manager. Theodore. The man stealing from Gunn. Had he found out that she'd uncovered his theft?

"What is it Gunn has ye working on? I ken he gave ye employment. Doing what?"

She snatched her arm back and jutted out her chin.

"I do not believe that is any concern of yours. If you'll excuse me." She moved to enter her room, but he blocked the way.

"I believe I asked ye a question," he snarled, his eyes almost black in color.

"And *I* believe that I do not have to answer your question."

Stalking forward, she couldn't help but step back until she was flush against the wall.

"Listen," he warned, his hands lifted to the wall, enclosing her as if she were in a cage. "I have kenned Gunn a long time. Much longer than ye. I warn ye against snooping around places ye shouldna be."

"Are you threatening me? I'm sure Gunn would not appreciate such an action."

He dropped his arms and stepped back, a sneer marring his face. "I would ne'er threaten a lady. But ye arena one, are ye?" he snapped. "Heed my warning." Then he turned and disappeared quickly down the stairs.

Jocelyn placed her palm over her heart, it beat so fast under her hand. She took a deep breath and blew out slowly through her mouth, trying to calm herself. And repeated the action before entering her room and locking the door behind her.

Theodore was definitely scared of her uncovering his secret. Sadly, for him, it was far too late for that since not only had she done exactly that, Gunn was well aware of what he had been doing.

Gunn.

She should talk to him in the morning about Theodore's visit. Or mayhap not. She sighed as she sat on her bed, contemplating what she should do. In the morning she'd decide what to do. For now, she wanted to get lost in happy memories.

Reaching into the drawer of the bedside table, she pulled out her mother's diary and paged to the section where she wrote about meeting her father for the first time. The entry was endearing. She talked about how dashing he was. Courteous. Gentlemanly. She wrote that she knew she would marry him from that very first meeting. It was as if all the stars had aligned in just the right way bringing them together.

It kind of matched up with the way Jocelyn had met Gunn. Serendipity perhaps. The universe was in alignment that night.

She wished her parents were still here. She missed them so much. She also believed they would have supported her in the actions she'd taken to get away from Victor. Would have actively joined forces with Gunn to remove Victor from her and the babe's life.

Lying down, she snuggled into the pillow. Thoughts of Gunn meeting her parents. They would have liked him. Approved of him. She was sure of that.

As she slipped into a blissful sleep, images of Gunn holding her babe floated behind her eyelids. All was good.

She could only hope it stayed that way.

CHAPTER TWELVE

The rest of the week passed uneventfully. Gunn and Jocelyn fell into an easy routine. He'd moved her desk into his study and set it up beside his.

He found that he got lonely when she wasn't near. And really, he was wrong in his decision to tuck her away into an old storage room.

They'd spoken regarding her employment and come to an agreement that they were no longer boss and employee. Thankfully. That never sat well with him anyway. But he had offered her what he thought she needed at the time.

Instead, she was reviewing his ledgers out of interest. It was clear now that Theodore was stealing from him. The man didn't have a clue that Jocelyn had uncovered his unsavory acts. They agreed to keep it that way.

For now.

When she'd told him of Theodore's visit, Gunn was ready to go to Theodore's house and show him with his fists what would happen when he threatened Jocelyn.

But she held him back. Reminding him that she hadn't finished her review yet. That there might be more items to uncover.

He sighed.

Gunn needed to wait until he and his friends were together and come up with a plan of action. For now, he was biding his time. Keeping a close eye on Theodore and questioning every act he did and word he said. Even more so now.

Currently, Theodore was taking stock of the pub's inventory.

It pissed Gunn off. He didn't want the louse anywhere near his pub, let alone taking inventory, and sure as hell not anywhere near Jocelyn.

"It looks like we are going to need to order more scotch," Theodore called from behind the bar.

"Dinna we have some in storage?" Gunn was quite sure they did. It took extra effort to keep his face neutral when he spoke to his once trusted friend.

"I dinna believe so. I clearly remember grabbing the last bottle. Mayhap we should place a large order to save on cost," Theodore suggested.

Gunn harrumphed. *I'm sure he would like that.* "I canna afford a large order."

Theodore approached the table where Gunn sat. "I ken funds are tight. But ye have to remember ye have more assets at your fingertips."

"Nay. My estate finances are separate. I will no' mix the two," he stated for the umpteenth time. Gunn could only assume since Theodore bled the pub dry, that he now wanted to get his hands on Gunn's estate finances. Thankfully, when he'd put him in charge of the Thistle & Pig he hadn't also charged him with his estate upkeep. If he had, there was no doubt that Theodore would be pilfering what he could from there as well. Which, as of now, was naught. But he wasn't going to let Theodore ken that. Let him keep believing that he had lots of money in his other properties.

He didn't ken why his longtime *friend* wanted to bankrupt him, but he wouldn't allow it. Nay longer. He'd done enough damage to his business. And when he got to the bottom of his scheme, Gunn would ensure he would be unable to find employment in all of Scotland.

"I understand 'tis no ideal, but what will ye do if ye canna serve scotch to your patrons? 'Tis your most popular offering."

He narrowed his eyes at Theodore, assessing him, but not saying a word. Thoughts of punching that smirk off his face hit him hard and he shook his head to clear the image.

The man seemed to shrink under his scrutiny. Eyes darting around the pub nervously.

Aye. Theodore was definitely up to no good. How had Gunn not seen it before? His friend was shifty. Nervous.

Mayhap he was so wrapped up in trying to figure out why people stopped coming that he didn't notice his friend's change in demeanor.

And whilst the lack of customers surely had an impact on why no money was coming in, why had they stopped coming? Had Theodore done something to make them stop coming so he could use that as an excuse as to why there was no money?

Could it really be that simple? It would indeed be a simple, yet conniving, plan.

"I'll have Thomas get a bottle of scotch. Only the one. I canna afford any more."

"Surely, one bottle willna be enough. Let me take care of it. 'Tis my job."

Gunn lifted a brow in question. "Is it? 'Tis your job to ensure we have patrons, but yet, looking around, I dinna see any. Do ye?"

Theodore laughed nervously. "Nay, but 'tis early still."

"Aye, my dining room should be full of patrons who are breaking their fast after staying the night in my inn, but alas, that is also empty."

"Ye have one customer," he chided.

"If ye are referring to Jocelyn, ye can damn well take those words back and ye well ken it."

Theodore put his hands up in defense. "I am just saying. Isna it funny how she arrived on your doorstep, out of the several inns in this town, asking for free lodging and food? Seems suspicious to me." He shrugged as if he hadn't just insulted Gunn's intelligence.

He wouldn't have Theodore speaking ill of Jocelyn.

"Ye are dismissed for the day."

"Excuse me? Ye canna be serious."

"I am. I can run my own pub for the day. And I suggest that if ye want to stay employed in this establishment, that ye mind your words when speaking of Jocelyn."

Dawning widened Theodore's eyes. "Ye two." He waved his hands in the air. "Ye two. Are together? Ye're courting her?"

"Tisna any of your business what we are doing. Now leave before I have the mind to remove ye myself." He would take immense pleasure in doing so.

"Fine. Ye want me to leave for the day? I shall. But I think ye need to get your affairs in order, Gunn." He pointed his index finger at him. "Ye are running out of resources and unless ye start pulling them from your estate, ye're going to lose your pub and inn. No bonny lass will save it."

Gunn stood, pushing his chair back with such force it toppled over.

Theodore's eyes rounded as he noticed Gunn's clenched fists and put his hands up in defense.

"I'm going. Ye can relax."

He watched Theodore exit through the door, catching the sneer he threw back before disappearing down the street. He wanted naught more than to kick him out of the Thistle & Pig for good, but he couldn't. Not yet.

His earlier thoughts gave him an idea. It was time he went out into the town and talked to the people to find out why they stopped frequenting his business.

Even better, he could use the time to walk with Jocelyn on his arm.

He found Jocelyn and Lizzie playing a game of cribbage in the salon.

"Hello ladies," he called out. "Who's winning?"

They looked up at his voice and Jocelyn smiled widely. He

couldn't help but return the smile. It was the same every time he was in her presence. He couldn't stop himself from smiling widely.

"I am," Jocelyn answered, clapping her hands excitedly.

"Calm down," Lizzie drawled. "'Tis beginner's luck."

"I think not. It's because I had a great teacher." Jocelyn giggled and turned to him. "I had never played cribbage before. Lizzie taught me. It's fun!"

"I'm glad ye're enjoying it. I wondered if ye cared for a walk or shall I come back later?"

"My legs could use a stretch, and the fresh air will do me some good. Lizzie, do you want to join us?"

"Nay. Ye two go on. I'm waiting for Malcolm and hopefully, he'll arrive soon."

"I am certain he misses ye as well, Lizzie," Gunn offered.

"I didna say I missed him."

Gunn laughed. "Ye didna have to, 'tis written all o'er your face."

She blushed. "Shush. Ye two go." She stood and gestured them toward the door. "Enjoy your walk."

Outside, the air was crisp but pleasant. Jocelyn had her hand tucked into the crook of his elbow. As they strolled down the street, he kenned what they looked like to passersby—a couple. And he liked that very much.

Clearing his throat, he spoke. "I must confess, I had an ulterior motive for this walk."

"Oh?" A flash of worry crossed Jocelyn's face before she quickly masked it.

"Dinna fash, lass. 'Tis naught bad. When I was speaking with Theodore earlier, he was trying to get me to use my estate finances to pay for inventory for the pub. Something that, as ye ken, I couldna do e'en if I wanted to. But he doesna ken that. It got me thinking that since he's emptied the Thistle & Pig's coffers that he needed me to get money from other sources that he could syphon."

"That makes sense."

He nodded. "Aye, but one thing that I canna wrap my head around is the patrons. Why they stopped coming? I understand him stealing the money. He's obviously using it for something. What? I have no idea. But wouldn't he want the pub to be filled with customers so he could continue stealing?

"But then it occurred to me that he may have had a hand in ensuring the townsfolk went elsewhere. I think he believed that I wouldna uncover his deception if they stopped coming. No one coming in, the money dries up."

"That's dastardly. Do you really think he'd go to such measures?"

"I no longer ken what to believe. I ne'er thought he would steal from me, but he has."

"So, what does this walk have to do with all that?"

The wind picked up and she cinched her cloak tighter.

"Are ye cold? We can return to the inn to get ye inside by the fire."

She smiled. "Your concern is endearing, but I'm fine." She patted his arm. "Go on. Tell me this plan of yours."

"I want to talk to the people in town. Ask why they've stopped coming in."

"Do you think they will speak so candidly to you?"

He shrugged. "I dinna ken. But I must try. I need to learn the reason so I can reverse it. Whate'er Theodore's plan is, I plan to thwart it."

They spent the next hour interviewing people around town. Folks that used to frequent the pub and inn often and one thing was for certain.

Theodore had done a thorough job making them believe that the pub, the inn, and everything contained within were a hazard in one way or another and both were on the brink of closing.

The bastard.

Another common answer was that they had been referred to another establishment on the other side of town. When asking who owned it, they couldn't answer. They'd never met the man.

Gunn had the sinking feeling that the owner was Theodore and the money he'd stolen from the Thistle & Pig had gone into making that pub successful.

Gunn wasn't much of a charmer, but he soon realized Jocelyn was. With her insistence that the Thistle & Pig was better than ever, and her encouragement for them to return, many of his former patrons promised to be back.

"Ye were brilliant," Gunn complimented Jocelyn as they entered the inn. "Everyone loved ye, but how could they no'?" he added with a wink.

"I don't know about that, but I am glad to help. Your place is lovely and deserves to be as successful as it was before."

"Willna Theodore be surprised to see a full bar when people start to return? I look forward to seeing his expression."

"What are you going to do about his place?"

"Now that we ken the name of it, when everyone is here, we will pay it a visit. Until then, I will remain mum."

Inside, Gunn helped Jocelyn out of her cloak. Laughter from down the hall greeted them.

"It sounds like Malcolm has returned. Which reminds me. There's something I want to ask ye." Dropping his hands on her waist, he pulled her close.

With her hands on his shoulders, she tipped up her face to meet his eyes. "Yes?" she said, her voice husky, and he kenned she was waiting for him to kiss her. Which he gladly would. He just had one question first.

"In the next day or two everyone is gathering at my estate. Join me?"

Her eyes rounded. "I don't want to intrude."

"Dinna be silly." He tugged her closer. "I want ye there." He bent and captured her lips in a soft kiss, savoring how she melded into him.

Her arms looped around his neck, and he never wanted her to let go.

They broke the kiss, and she smiled slyly.

"Well, how can I reject that request?"

※※※※※

JOCELYN WAS PACKING her few belongings in her bag when a knock sounded. "Come in."

Flora poked her head in. "My lady, ye received a delivery from Madame Gossard."

Her new gowns. Just in time for her to bring them to Gunn's estate. She breathed a sigh of relief. She had been worrying about how she would be received by his friends when they realized she only owned two gowns. Lizzie had tried to reassure her that they weren't like that, but it didn't stop her from worrying still.

"There are multiple packages. It appears that ye will have a full wardrobe."

Jocelyn watched in amazement as Flora stacked the items on the bed. She hadn't realized she had ordered so much. Had she?

Lizzie appeared in the doorway. "Your new gowns have arrived I heard. I canna wait to see how they came out."

Flora curtsied and left the room.

"Go on," Lizzie urged. "Unbox them."

They opened package after package. Oohing and aahing after each reveal.

Madame Gossard had outdone herself. Every item was of the highest quality, with unique details that ensured no one else would have the same gown.

"Ye must wear this one this eve when we all gather for dinner." Lizzie picked up a gown that matched the color of the roses that used to grow in her mother's garden. "It's beautiful."

Jocelyn studied the piece. It was a delicate balance between pink and red, the color rich with matching beading that lined the hem of the sleeves. A pair of slippers to match had the same beading stitched into a rose pattern on the toe.

"Speaking of that. Is everyone gathering here or are we all meeting at Gunn's estate?"

"There, I believe. They will all have been traveling for some time, and it will be better for them to have time to settle in in one place."

Jocelyn nodded, worrying her lip.

"Are ye still nervous about meeting everyone? Dinna be. Ye won o'er Gunn. If ye can do that, ye will have no problem with the others."

"I hope so. I am nervous, but also excited, if that makes sense. You and Gunn talk so fondly of the others that I am looking forward to meeting them."

"I'm glad. They're bringing the wee ones, too. 'Twill be a fun time." She moved to the door. "I need to go and finish packing our stuff. If I leave it to Malcolm everything will be in a rumpled heap when we arrive." She giggled and then she was gone.

Looking at the pile of gowns, slippers, undergarments, a cloak, and new bonnets, Jocelyn didn't know how she would get it all packed. The bag she'd arrived with surely wouldn't accommodate everything.

She would have to track down Gunn and ask if he had an extra travel trunk she could borrow.

She found him in the pub, wiping down a table as he chatted with Thomas. There were more people inside then she'd ever seen since she'd been here. It was a lovely sight to see. A wide smile broke out on her face, she was so happy for Gunn.

Someone called his name, and he sauntered over to the table, laughter erupted, and he clapped the man on the back. Noticing her there, he smiled, threw the towel over his shoulder and approached.

"Can ye believe it?" He nodded his head in the direction of the filled tables. "It's much the same in the dining room."

"It's wonderful. You going out into town to talk to everyone appears to have paid off."

"Aye. Theodore is seething mad, though he's trying to mask it. I'm just playing daft like I havena any idea why people are returning."

She laughed. "Won't he figure it out?"

Gunn shrugged, his massive shoulders straining the seams of his white linen shirt. "I dinna ken. He hasna yet. Which is good. I dinna want him to ken that I'm aware of his antics until I and my friends show up at the bar he owns. I'm certain he will show his face then."

She bumped him with her shoulder. "You are evil."

He tapped her nose. "I am no', but if I were, I am your evil." He kissed her on the cheek.

Jocelyn looked around to gage people's reactions, but no one paid them any attention.

"Did ye need aught?"

"Oh, yes. The modiste delivered my new gowns amongst other things."

"Great. Just in time. How did they come out?"

"Lovely. They are all beautiful. Her talent is unmatched. Though I believe there are more items than I had spoken to her about."

Gunn grinned wide. "I wanted to ensure ye had plenty."

What a sweet gesture. He'd gone to the modiste after she'd been? "That is very kind of you. One problem though."

He frowned. "What is wrong? I will have her fix it straightaway."

"No, no. As I said everything is lovely. But I don't have anything to pack them in. My travel bag is much too small. Do you have an extra travel trunk I can borrow?"

"Borrow? Nay. But I have one ye can have."

She ducked her head shyly. She still wasn't used to being treated so well. "Thank you."

"I'll bring it up shortly. Will that work?"

"Of course. Whenever is convenient for you." She turned to leave but spun around again. "What time are we leaving this afternoon?"

"The ride isna long, but I would like to leave around noon. Will that be acceptable?"

Other than packing, she didn't have any other plans. "Of course."

He nodded. "I'll be up shortly with the trunk."

"Thank you."

She really felt like she was living in some sort of fairy tale like her father used to tell her when she was young. This type of relationship was what she had expected with Victor. Her mood darkened at the thought. Wariness still hung heavy on her shoulders whenever his name entered her mind. There was a possibility that he could still find her. What would happen then?

Legally, they were still married. What she was doing with Gunn was wrong. She knew it. Gunn knew it but cared not about the ramifications. He'd mentioned his friends were well seated and would help her through the situation. She only hoped they got a chance to work everything out before Victor found her.

Certainly, she didn't want him to find out about the babe. She wanted him to stay as far away from their baby as possible.

Back in her room, she folded everything neatly so that it would take up as little space as possible in the trunk. Even so, with the number of items, she wondered if one trunk would be enough. It had to be. She would make it work. The last thing she wanted to be deemed was difficult and needy.

"I've got your trunk," Gunn called from the hallway, and she rushed to open the door to let him in. He entered and set the trunk beside the bed, his eyes scanning the piles of folded clothing.

"Thank you. It shouldn't take me long to get these packed and then I'll be ready."

He smiled, and tugged on her arm, pulling her closer. He sat on the trunk and for a moment she worried that he would split it in two with his heft, but it remained intact.

She settled between his open legs, and he rested his hands on her hips. "I've been waiting for this all morn." He pulled her down so she was sitting on his lap and pushed her hair behind her ears, his fingers tracing the shell of her ear, then trailing down the column of her throat.

Her breath hitched as he nuzzled her neck.

"Mmm, lass, ye smell divine."

"It's cinnamon soap. From the mercantile," she said breathlessly.

"Ye smell good enough to eat."

She gasped at his forwardness.

"But alas, there isna time as we will be leaving shortly." He lifted her off his lap and stood stiffly, but not before she felt his hardness.

She pressed her lips together to stop from giggling.

"Howe'er, once we get to Leyson? Ye are all mine," his voice was low, sending shivers down her spine.

Suddenly, she couldn't wait for them to be on their way.

She looked forward to being all his.

CHAPTER THIRTEEN

GUNN HAD TO leave the room for fear he would take Jocelyn right then and there. He wanted to. Och, he ached to do so. But he would wait.

She longed for him as much as he longed for her. She hadn't said the words, but they showed in every action. Every look. Every sigh.

Once they arrived at Leyson, he made no promises as to how much self-control he would have. He wanted to get lost in her body for days in his own bedchamber. One that he would share with her.

Things needed to be taken care of first. The priority was her husband. Malcolm had made some headway before Gunn had called him back. He'd found their house in Rochester. Victor wasn't there of course. As Jocelyn had mentioned, he had gone south to look for her.

According to his house staff, he was furious when he'd learned she'd run. He'd left in a tizzy and hadn't returned yet.

He'd asked around the city to see what people thought about Jocelyn, but no one seemed to really ken her. She was rarely seen outside of the home. But when they did interact with her, she seemed nice, but quiet, reserved. She didn't participate in any of the activities that other wives did. No bridge clubs or afternoon teas.

It angered Gunn to find out this information. It was like the louse was holding her prisoner in her own home. Though he was sure much of the reason why he kept her hidden was so that others in the city didn't see the constant bruises she wore. Because it was obvious to him, that she was constantly bruised and battered.

Malcolm said the house was modest. Not large, but not small, either. It was well kept, and he employed a full staff, though none would speak of Jocelyn other than to say how angry Victor was when he'd found her gone.

Gunn would ensure she would never have reason to fear him. He vowed that on his life. And he'd give his before he would see her hurt again. He couldn't change her past, but he could make sure that her future was only filled with love and happiness.

Malcolm caught him in the hall. "The carriages are ready. Once the ladies are finished their packing we can load the trunks and be on our way."

"Jocelyn shouldna be much longer. The poor lass only had a small travel bag when she arrived. I had to bring her a trunk for her new wardrobe."

"Ye are completely smitten with her. Lizzie was right."

His friend wasn't wrong. Gunn didn't even bother trying to deny it any longer. He shrugged. "It all feels right."

"She's still married legally," Malcolm warned. "E'en if she ran and her husband is a useless arse. The law wins on this one."

"I ken that," he snapped. He scrubbed his face, then pinched the bridge of his nose. "Sorry. I didna mean to be short. I understand the situation. 'Tis why I need all of us to get together and help me figure out how to solve it."

"What are we going to do?"

"I dinna ken, but five minds are better than one, and between all of us, certainly we can come up with some viable plan."

"Ye are daft."

"Am I? If I recall, ye traveled the countryside to prove the innocence of a woman ye'd just met."

"Hey. E'en ye have to admit she didn't look like a thief."

"True, but would I have done what ye did? I canna say for sure, but probably no'." He barked out a laugh and Malcolm punched him in the shoulder.

"The first thing I want to do when we get to Leyson is a few rounds of boxing. 'Tis been too long since I've been in the ring. And my pub has been empty for so long I havena e'en been able to toss anyone out there. Though that looks to be changing now."

Malcolm laughed. "The way ye're wound up, I'll let Alexander take ye on. He can always use a good smackdown."

"I'm finally packed," Jocelyn announced, joining them and settling into Gunn's side. He brought his arm around her shoulders.

"That was quick. Malcolm and I will go get the trunks when Lizzie has finished."

Once the trunks were loaded onto the carriages and they were ready to go, Gunn turned to Jocelyn. "All set?" She was wearing a day gown of light blue that nearly matched her eyes, a satin sash tied at her waist. He splayed his palms on her still flat stomach.

Her eyes tracked his hands.

"I canna believe ye have a wee bairn growing in there."

She smiled, a touch of sadness in her eyes. It irked him every time. A bairn was something to celebrate. And he hated that it was a reminder of her husband's cruelty.

"That bairn will have the happiest of lives, lass. We will make sure of it."

She nodded. "I know." Reaching up, she palmed his cheek. "You are the greatest man I've ever met, outside of my father of course."

"Of course," he smiled. "I've got big shoes to fill when it comes to him."

"You are well on your way."

He clasped her hand and brought it to his mouth, placing a kiss on her soft skin. "Let's get to Leyson. I do hope ye like it."

"I've no doubt I will."

"I just need to go in and check one last time with Thomas and Theodore. I'll be back in just a minute, then we'll go."

Inside, he found Thomas pouring a whisky for Smythe.

"A minute?" He gestured for Thomas to join him near the back of the pub. "I ken ye can handle e'erything on your own. I've nay doubt in that. I'm no' that far away if aught comes up. Send for me."

He didn't need to expand further on what he was talking about. He'd let Thomas ken that he had suspicions of Theodore only to find out his bartender had thought that for some time.

If he noticed Theodore doing aught out of sorts whilst he was gone, he was going to send for him straightaway. Luckily, today was the last day of his week, and he wasn't scheduled for next week, so Thomas only had to worry about tonight.

That also meant that when Gunn and his friends went to the pub he was certain Theodore owned, he would be there.

"Dinna fash. I can handle it," Thomas assured him. "Ye enjoy your time away. 'Tis well deserved."

He found Theodore near the entrance that led to the inn. "Are ye set for the rest of the day? We're ready to head to Leyson."

Theodore nodded as his eyes scanned the pub. "I dinna ken what happened," he said with disbelief.

Gunn smiled and clapped him on the back. "'Tis great is it no'? A miracle I must say."

"'Tis indeed. I am glad to see it."

The man was lying through his teeth, but Gunn let it go. His comeuppance was on its way. And he couldn't wait to deliver it.

WHEN GUNN SPOKE about his estate at Leyson, Jocelyn figured it was large considering he was bringing all his friends and their families there, but when the carriage pulled into the long drive that led to Leyson, her mouth dropped open in shock.

Leyson was a castle.

Gunn owned a castle. On the shores of the North Sea, the structure loomed tall and massive. Grey stone stood at least four stories high with turrets at every corner.

"Wow," she whispered, taking it all in. "You didn't say Leyson was a castle."

He squeezed her knee. "Sorry, I ne'er call it Leyson Castle. I always just refer to it as Leyson."

The way he talked was as if it was just any homestead. That it was something ordinary when it was quite the opposite.

They finally pulled up to the front of the house and staff swarmed outside to greet their laird.

Beside her, he stiffened. Immediately, she understood that he much preferred the laid-back setting of the Thistle & Pig. That was probably why he spent so much time there. It got him away from his duties as laird and not having to be as proper.

What those duties were she had no idea, but she could only assume there were many. She couldn't imagine how much work it was to maintain a residence of this size.

A footman approached the carriage and opened the door as it rocked to a stop. "My laird, welcome home," he said with a bow.

Gunn exited and turned to offer her a hand to help her out.

Malcolm and Lizzie were right behind them.

Right away, Lizzie looped her arm into hers. "I canna wait for ye to meet everyone." Her hair was slightly out of place and her cheeks were flushed, her lips swollen.

Jocelyn hid her smile behind her hand. It didn't take a genius to figure out how they'd spent their journey.

"Did you enjoy the ride?" Jocelyn asked, her voice teasing.

"We did indeed." Lizzie waggled her brows. "Did ye?"

Jocelyn smiled, nodding. "Whilst our journey was much more, ahem, uneventful, we had pleasant conversation."

"We had pleasant conversation," Lizzie mimicked. "Ye two make me laugh. I dinna believe Gunn didn't make more creative use of the time alone with ye."

"Lizzie!" Jocelyn playfully pushed her shoulder. "Don't say such things."

With a roll of her eyes, Lizzie shook her head. "Ye ken 'tis going to happen."

"Oh, it will, yes. But it will be in the comfort of the laird's bedroom," she confided, giggling uncontrollably.

Now it was Lizzie's turn to gasp. "Jocelyn! Ye must tell me e'erything. Or wait until I introduce ye to the others. Then you can tell *us* e'erything."

Jocelyn's insecurity ramped up once again. She wasn't so sure that conversation should be the first topic they discuss upon meeting.

"We're going inside to meet the others since ye two are out here lallygagging about."

Gunn met her eyes, his dancing with laughter. "We are right behind ye two. No need to sass us, Lizzie."

She heard him turn to Malcolm and comment how he didn't know how he dealt with his wife. All in good nature, of course. Both men laughed behind them as they walked through the arched entry and through the courtyard that would lead them inside.

As soon as they entered, the sound of laughter filled the air, along with the stomping feet of little ones. Jocelyn smiled. Her excitement was growing to meet the people in Gunn's life that he held in such high regard. She was still nervous, but he'd spoken about them enough that she felt like she almost knew them. He'd insisted repeatedly that they would like her. Actually, he said they would love her. She wasn't sure about that, but she would settle for being liked and accepted in the group of close-knit friends.

They climbed the stairs, using the excited noises to lead their way. They found everyone in the drawing room. Jocelyn was taken aback at how quickly everyone stopped and assessed her.

"E'eryone," Lizzie announced. "Meet Jocelyn Townsend, Gunn's," she glanced at him over her shoulder. "Well, they're courting for the most part, so call their relationship what ye will," she said with a laugh. She pointed to a petite woman with kind eyes. She held a babe on one hip while she tried to hold onto a tot as he tried to wrestle free from her grasp. "This is Gwen, she's married to Nicholas. Duke and Duchess of Gordon."

Jocelyn's eyes widened and she immediately dropped into a curtsy. "Your graces."

Gwen handed the babe to her husband. With a smile, he grabbed the babe and nuzzled her neck, causing a deep belly laugh. One side of the duke's face was marred with scars, but it did nothing to take away from his handsomeness. With kind eyes, he greeted her with a dip of his head.

"Please," Gwen said, approaching and wrapping Jocelyn in a hug. "Amongst friends, there are no titles. I'm Gwen and he's Nicholas. Simple as that."

Jocelyn wasn't sure if she would feel comfortable referring to them by their first names, but then Gunn was a laird, and she'd been calling him by his first name this whole time.

"We are very informal. There's no need for all that stuffiness. 'Tis nice to meet ye."

"You as well. Thank you."

"Ye're English," Gwen stated matter-of-factly. "I look forward to how ye ended up here. These two wee ones are Benjamin, but we call him Bennie, and Violet. And this one," she pointed to her round belly, we havena decided yet."

"Congratulations. You are very blessed."

"We are," Nicholas said, bending to kiss Gwen's cheek. "I'll take the wee ones. Ye have fun getting acquainted."

A dark-haired woman approached, and Jocelyn noted her coloring and features mirrored Nicholas's. "I'm Clarissa, Nicholas's sister in case ye havena guessed. My husband, Alexander, is the one wisecracking o'er in the corner. He's got a sharp tongue but it's all in good fun. I'm glad to meet the woman who captured Gunn's heart. Honestly, I didna think 'twould e'er happen."

"It's nice to meet you. If I'm not mistaken you are the Duke and Duchess of Argyll, correct?"

"Aye, but as Gwen said, titles mean naught when we're together. Our wee laddie, Colin, is down for a nap. Ye'll ken when he's awake, he chitters more than a lassie." She laughed and gestured for her husband to join Nicholas as he left.

"Since it seems we men are being ushered out of the room, I shall make a quick introduction. Finlay Primrose. 'Tis a pleasure to meet ye. I'm sure ye and my wife, Willamina, will get on splendidly." A woman, heavily pregnant, pushed off the sofa she'd been sitting on and greeted her with a smile, her hands on her back.

"Dinna mind me. I am slow moving around." She pointed to Finlay. "And this one willna let me do aught. I nearly had to beg to get him to agree to this trip."

"Aye, what if the bairn comes?" he asked, concern creasing his brow.

"Then we visit a wee bit longer," she answered with a laugh.

Finlay shook his head. "I'll be with the others. Call me if ye need me." He dropped his lips to hers. "I miss ye already."

"Stop," she said, but her voice was laced with laughter.

After the men had left the room, all eyes turned to Jocelyn, and she felt her cheeks flush. They pulled her onto the sofa where Willamina had been sitting, and was now once again, and they pulled chairs around to form a circle.

"We want all the details," they all said at the same time.

CHAPTER FOURTEEN

"Jocelyn's a bonnie lass," Alexander spoke once they'd all filed into Gunn's study.

"Ye have a wife and a wee one," Gunn stated but he was only jesting. Alexander was the one out of all of their friends that they thought would never settle down. None of them had realized he'd been pining for Nicholas's sister, nor that Clarissa had been for him either. But it was obvious once they'd seen each other.

"Ye have been busy growing your families. I am happy to see it. The ladies look happy and well loved. Nicholas, are ye trying to beat your parent's record?" Gunn chuckled.

Nicholas had six siblings that he cared for after their father had passed. Most could take care of themselves, but he had a set of twins on the younger side. Gwen had a brother their age, along with two others. Now with the addition of two wee ones and one on the way, Huntly Castle's walls were indeed full.

"We both said we wanted children. Why wait? Speaking of, Malcolm, what are ye waiting for?"

"Hey now," Malcolm chided. "If it happens, it happens. 'Tis no' for lack of trying on our end, if ye ken what I mean?"

"I ken verra well," Gunn murmured. "Did ye enjoy the ride o'er?"

Finlay barked out a laugh. "I love a good carriage ride." He waggled his eyebrows.

"Ye both are the worst. What would Lizzie and Willamina say if they heard ye speak of such things?"

"They would agree," Finlay and Malcolm said in unison.

"Let me bring these two to their nanny. They can use naps, then we can get down to business," Nicholas said as he stood.

"Come here, Bennie," Alexander called and scooped the tot up in his arms. "Uncle Alex will help your papa get ye and your wee sis to bed."

Malcolm nodded toward the door Nicholas and Alexander had just disappeared through. "Ye ready for that?" he asked Finlay.

"I canna wait. I tried to convince Willamina to stay home." He looked at Gunn. "No' because I didna want to come. She's so close. What would have happened if the bairn decided to come whilst we were traveling?"

"I would have understood, but I'm glad ye came. 'Tis been too long since we've all been together."

"Aye," Finlay agreed.

"I think we could all use a drink before we get down to serious talk." He stood and went over to the sideboard that was well-stocked with the finest whisky. As he poured the dark amber liquid into glasses, he thought about the bairns. Those already here and those on the way. Including Jocelyn's, wondering if she would have a lass that favored her mama's looks, or a lad that favored his papa's.

He frowned. Would he find that upsetting? There was a good chance that the bairn would look like their father. He shook the feeling away before it had time to fester. The bairn would be loved. And treated as if it were his own. The wee one would never ken any different.

"Are ye going to pass those out or just stand there like an oaf?" Malcolm asked, eyeing him suspiciously.

"Sorry."

"What are ye sorry for now?" Alexander asked as he walked in, Nicholas close behind.

"Apparently, I wasna passing out the whisky soon enough."

With drinks in hand, they all took a seat, their attention focused on Gunn. He sipped his drink, letting the liquid heat his throat.

"Ye ken the women are gossiping in the salon," Alexander said. "'Tis time for our own. Out with it. How did ye meet Jocelyn?"

Gunn went through the story of how she entered his pub that night and how she hadn't left since. How they were planning for their future.

"I need your help with a couple of things."

Nicholas grew serious. "Aught. Ye name it."

"Her husband is currently searching for her. 'Twill no' be long before he realizes she's escaped north instead of south as he originally thought."

"Are ye certain?" Finlay asked.

"Aye. Malcolm did some research before I learned the facts of Jocelyn's past. He's a bastard. I dinna think he'll let her go."

"Clearly, he canna love her if he treated her so poorly," Finlay offered.

Gunn scratched at his jaw, his stubble making his skin itch. He needed a shave. "'Tis all his ego, I believe. He sees her as property. Naught more."

"Bastard," Alexander spat. "'Tis good she found ye."

Shrugging, he scraped his hand over his mouth. "We need to find a way to make him agree to a divorce. I dinna care if I have to pay the arsehole off. Whate'er needs to be done, I'll do it."

"Sounds serious." It was Nicholas. His friend was usually quiet. Serious. But loyal to a fault. "Are ye sure this is what ye want?"

Was it? He thought about when he was with Jocelyn. It was as if the rest of the world fell away, and it was only them there in the moment. No worries or cares. It was just them. Drinking each other in.

He nodded. "I'm certain."

"I dinna believe it," Alexander said. "Ye, the last holdout from our group of friends, is finally settling down. With an English woman, no less."

"Where she was born has naught to do with it, ye sod."

"What's the plan? Are we going to Rochester? Track him down? Or wait for him to show up here?"

"I havena decided. But there's something else I need help with."

Serious looks on his friends' faces let him ken that whatever it was he needed, they were there for him. The same as he'd been there for them when they needed something. It was what friends did. Helped each other whenever one needed it. They'd been so close growing up. Played together. Served together. Supported each other. Now it was his turn to draw on their collective help.

He stood, refilled his whisky, and held up the bottle for whoever else needed more. All except Finlay raised their glass and Gunn kenned it was because his friend wanted to keep a clear head in case the bairn decided to enter the world.

Pacing the floor, he swallowed his pride and told his friends about the financial hardships he had been facing with the Thistle & Pig.

"When Jocelyn asked for employment, the only thing I could think of was ledger review. I had been meaning to do it but kept pushing it off. It was a task I loathed and I was too focused on trying to bring the pub and inn back to life."

"That's understandable given the stress ye were under. But why would ye have her assessing your books?" Alexander asked. "Ye'd just met her, and she's a woman."

Gunn laughed, pointed a finger at his friend. "Aye, but a smart one at that. Her father taught her accounting as a way of ensuring she would have the knowledge to care for her own finances when she married," he scoffed. "The bastard took all of that from her."

"So no' only was he violent against her, he couldna stand for her to be independent thinking?"

"Exactly, Finlay. The last thing he wanted was for her to ken what he was doing with the money." He sipped his whisky, emptying the glass so he placed it on his desk. "Whilst she was reviewing my ledgers she uncovered some unaccounted transactions. Long story short, Theodore has been stealing from my coffers and practically bankrupting my business."

"What the hell?" Alexander spat.

"The louse," Finlay snapped.

"Aye. No' only that, he was the reason that e'eryone stopped frequenting the pub and inn. Rumors were spread that somehow managed to stay out of my ears. Jocelyn and I went on a walk a few days ago and talked to people around town and found that to be the case. I dinna think it was him directly, but word got out. Jocelyn was verra convincing in getting the townsfolk to agree to return."

"Have they?" Nicholas asked.

Gunn nodded, sinking back into his chair. "'Tis only been a couple of days, but today the pub was filling up and patrons were once again filling the dining room at the inn. So much so, that I had to scramble to bring in help for Thomas and Flora. 'Twas too many people for them to handle themselves."

"That's great news, aye?" Alexander asked.

Agreeing, Gunn nodded. "I had to let so many people go, 'tis nice to ken that I will be able to hire a full staff back. That I will have the funds coming in to support them."

"How did Theodore react?" Finlay asked.

"No' well. He's trying to act happy about it, but I see through his façade."

"What can we do?" Alexander asked, leaning forward with his forearms on his thighs.

"It appears the money he was pilfering was to fund his own establishment. His plan to bankrupt no' only the Thistle & Pig, but my estate as well, was so that he could get rid of what he considered his number one competition."

"Nay," Alexander muttered in disbelief.

"Aye. I want all of us to go to his pub. Together as a banded front. I want to see the fear in his eyes when he realizes I am aware of what he's done."

"Och. 'Tis been some time since I've been in a fight, but I am ready." Nicholas stated.

The four men looked at him, surprise clear on their faces.

He put his hands up in defense. "What?" He pointed to his scars. "I am great at putting the fear of God into people. Especially no-good bastards."

Laughter erupted in the room.

"'Twill be like the old days," Finlay said.

Gunn clapped his hands. "All right, 'tis settled. We have dinner this eve, but on the morrow, we'll pay Theodore a visit.

Happy to have the support of his friends, he smiled, and they made a plan to leave at noon tomorrow.

"'Tis almost time for dinner. We should collect our wives and get ready," Malcolm said.

Gunn had no complaints about that. He couldn't wait to see Jocelyn again and see how she was faring with the other ladies. He had no doubt all went well, but she had been so nervous. He wanted to hear all about it.

FOUR SETS OF eyes focused on Jocelyn and the attention caused her heart to jump in her throat. Did they really just expect her to blurt out everything? About her and her past. About Gunn? It didn't seem proper to give such details to women she'd just met.

"Dinna be shy," Lizzie urged. "They dinna bite, and we all have pasts that arena the purest."

Jocelyn raised an eyebrow, curious of what Lizzie referred to. Two of the women that sat in front of her were duchesses. Certainly, their pasts were squeaky clean.

"I dinna ken she believes that, Lizzie," Clarissa pointed out. "Ye have spent the most time together. Did ye tell her how ye met Malcolm?"

She had. "Yes, they met at a ball," Jocelyn answered.

The women burst out in laughter.

Willamina clutched her stomach as she laughed so hard, tears shone in her eyes. "Aye, and I met Finlay at a garden party."

"Well, actually," Gwen said, "that is true."

Jocelyn laughed nervously. "I'm sorry, I fear that I am not privy to all of the background information you are." She turned to Lizzie, hurt a little that the person she had believed was fast becoming her friend, had lied to her. "You didn't meet at a ball?" she asked quietly.

Lizzie threw an annoyed look to Willamina. "We did meet at a ball, just no' in the conventional sense, I suppose."

"Did he not ask you to dance?"

Lizzie laughed. "He most definitely did not. He found me in the chamber of the viscountess that was hosting the party."

Jocelyn was confused. It still sounded to her as if they met at the ball.

"Malcolm was there to work. He was hired as security to ensure no one stole the viscountess's jewels. He found me with my hands in her jewelry chest."

Her mouth dropped open in shock. "You were stealing from the viscountess."

Willamina barked out a laugh, and Clarissa and Gwen shushed her.

"Nay. I was *retrieving* the jewelry of my grandmama that had been stolen from my family." She emphasized the word retrieving. "Anyhow, he didna believe me when I said they were mine. I did manage to convince him to follow me home to Stonehaven though, so I could prove it. Which I did. But I did meet him at a ball."

That was a lot of information to take in. Jocelyn couldn't imagine being mistaken for a thief. She would have been scared to death of losing a hand. Or being thrown into jail. Forced to work hard labor to pay back the sum of what she'd stolen.

"Um," Jocelyn muttered, scratching her ear. "I really don't know how to respond to that."

Giggles filled the room. "We all have our stories," Clarissa chimed in. "I was enamored with Alexander, much to my brother's chagrin and he did e'erything in his power to keep us apart."

"Nicholas caught me stealing flowers from his garden. And aye, I was really stealing them," Gwen confessed.

Once again, Jocelyn's jaw dropped.

"And Finlay and I did meet at a garden party, verra briefly. But we soon realized that we both had problems that needed solving, and the only solution was to get married right away."

"Did you love each other?"

Willamina slapped her knee with a guffaw. "I found him quite attractive, but love came later. And then I found out I was married twice."

The women laughed, and Jocelyn found that she couldn't stop herself from joining in with them. They weren't lying when they said they all had their own stories. She wanted to hear the gritty details of each one.

"I must admit that all of you are the opposite of what I expected. And I mean no offense by that whatsoever."

"See, ye were fashing for no reason," Lizzie offered.

"Now ye need to tell us how ye met Gunn," Gwen urged. "Ye ken all of our dark secrets." She rubbed her hands together, a wicked glint shining in her eyes. "Now we need to ken yours."

"Agreed," Willamina said, her hand drawing slow circles on her belly.

Jocelyn took a deep breath, and let it out in a huff, her hands resting on her knees. "I fear my story is nowhere close to all of yours when it comes to excitement."

"We shall be the judges of that," Clarissa laughed.

"I've run away from my husband," she blurted, and everyone but Lizzie, who already knew, gasped.

"Jocelyn!" Clarissa exclaimed. "How scandalous. Does he ken where ye are?"

She shook her head. "I don't believe so. Otherwise, he would have appeared. There was a reason I ran. I didn't just do it for fun or because I was bored."

"There's always a reason driving us forward in what we choose to do," Gwen said gently and Jocelyn got the feeling that she had been through a lot. "'Tis how we handle ourselves when the time comes that is important. To me, it sounds like ye did what ye had to do at the perfect time, leading ye to Gunn."

"I agree. However, I am still married, and this," she paused. What was it that she and Gunn were doing? What label did they give themselves? "Well, whatever it is that Gunn and I are doing goes against every vow I spoke when I married my husband."

On the sofa, Willamina straightened. "I believe I can speak on this as the only other one of us that has been married more than once. Ye need to do what is right for ye. Your husband was a cruel man, aye?"

Jocelyn nibbled at her lip, nodding.

"Mine was, too. In so many ways. When he died, I mourned him as was proper. But it wasna in a way that I missed him. It was as if a burden had been lifted. If I'm no' mistaken, I believe that is what ye are feeling now, is it no'?"

Jocelyn pondered her words. Relief had flooded her after the first night she'd left. Up until that time she was terrified that Victor would show up out of the blue, no matter where she was. When he hadn't, it was like light at the end of a long tunnel that she had to fight her way through.

The Thistle & Pig became her respite. Gunn her support.

"You're right. The time since I've left has been amazing. Gunn has been a big part of that, for which I will be forever grateful."

"If ye ask me, your arrival saved Gunn," Lizzie proclaimed.

"Well, I don't know about that."

"'Tis true. Ye dinna see him before. He was miserable. Grumpy all the time. Ye brought happiness and light back into his life. He needed that. Deserved that. And it sounds like ye did, too." Lizzie reached over and squeezed her hand.

"Och, look at the time," Gwen announced. "I suppose we should get ready for dinner. Mayhap after we can gather for games in the parlor?"

A round of ayes filled the room, along with Jocelyn's yes. It was funny how two countries, connected by land, had such different languages. She guessed it was the same for France and its nearby countries.

The women slowly exited the room, splintering off to different sections of Leyson depending on where their rooms were. She paused, trying to gain her bearings and remember which direction she needed to go to get to her room.

"Are ye lost?" a low voice rumbled behind her.

Gunn.

She smiled, turning and wrapping her arms around his neck. Stepping up on her tip toes, she kissed his cheek. "I must confess, I have no idea where I am or how to get back to my room." She stepped back, wetting her bottom lip with her tongue and looked up at him through her lashes. "Can you help me with that?"

He growled and nipped the air with his teeth. "I can definitely help ye."

With a warm hand at her back, he turned her in the opposite direction of where she thought she needed to go and led her down the hall and up the stairs.

"Your room is next to mine. I wanted ye to be close."

There was no denying what he meant by those words.

And lord above, forgive her, but she was excited by the thought of what was to come. Couldn't wait for it to happen.

CHAPTER FIFTEEN

WHEN GUNN SAW Jocelyn in the hall, looking confused, he wanted to scoop her up in his arms and carry her away to his room. Thoughts of spending the night there, whilst ignoring everyone else here was tempting. But he'd invited everyone so they could be together.

As tempting as the thought was, it would have to wait for another time. Having her as close as possible without her actually being in his room would suffice for now.

"I ken at the inn ye didna have the help ye needed. I apologize for that. To make up for it, I've assigned Louise to be your maid. She'll help ye with whate'er ye need."

"Flora was very helpful."

Gunn chuckled. "She is indeed. I dinna think I can e'er replace her."

He pushed open the door, and a deep sense of pride filled him when she looked around the room in awe.

"This is beautiful, and massive." She entered the room, spinning around, trying to take it all in.

"I am pleased that ye approve. All of your items should be unpacked. I will let Louise ken ye are here. She'll assist ye in getting ready for dinner."

Stepping up to him, she placed her palm on his chest, her fingers playing with his lapels. "Thank you. It seems your kindness knows no bounds."

"Ye deserve it all. I only hope I can make ye happy." Placing his hands on her waist, he pulled her closer. Dropped his head to capture his mouth with hers. She accepted willingly, her body melding to his.

His own body roared to life, seeking the release he'd been longing for since he'd first laid eyes on Jocelyn.

They broke the kiss with a sigh. "Dinner will be ready shortly. We shouldna be late." Then he remembered her worry from earlier. "How did it go with the ladies? Did ye get on well?"

She smiled, nodding her head. "Swimmingly, actually. They are all very kind and warm-hearted." She traced his cheek with a delicate finger. "They all care for you very much."

"I am glad to hear that your nerves were for naught. I figured as much, but one can ne'er be sure until placed into the situation. But I do recall telling ye that they would love ye."

Jocelyn rolled her eyes. "Right you were. I shouldn't have worried. They're lovely. I look forward to spending time getting to know all of them better."

That statement made him happy. It meant that she had no intention of leaving. He hadn't thought she did, but if she and the wives didn't get along, then it would have been hard to convince her to stay. Luckily, as expected, there was no issue.

"I'll let Louise ken to come up. I'll be back to escort ye to dinner, aye?"

She stood in the middle of the room, a smile on her lips, as she wrung her hands together. A gesture he noticed she did a lot. At first he thought it was just when she was nervous, but she did it so often that he didn't think that was the case.

"I would love that. Thank you."

He gave her a curt bow and left the room. Needing to get ready himself, he quickly found Louise and sent her to Jocelyn's room.

Back in his own room, he bathed the scent of the day's travel off and dressed in a clean linen shirt, blue trousers, and a matching waistcoat. Tying his cravat, he eyed himself in the looking glass. Never before had he cared so much about how his looks came across to other people. But now with Jocelyn, he couldn't stop. He wanted to ensure that he equaled her in dress.

He shook his head, mumbling to the empty room about the person he'd come to be.

One thing was for certain. He couldn't get the image of Jocelyn getting ready in the next room off his mind. Jocelyn in the bath, drops of water running in rivulets down her body, over her breasts, trailing down, lower, lower, until they disappeared into the water right before they could reach her nestle of curls.

Hell. God should strike him down now for coveting another man's wife, even if that so-called man didn't deserve to have Jocelyn in his life. Once again he thought about the impending showdown the two of them would have. Gunn was confident he would come out victorious, or rather, Jocelyn would. She was the one who deserved to be free. Deserved to make her own choices.

She'd already taken the first step by running. If only it was that easy.

He'd deal with Townsend and ensure he never again touched Jocelyn. That he didn't even look in her direction. Never thought of her again. Because one thing was for certain, Jocelyn was his.

And not because that was what he wanted, but because it was what she wanted.

After nursing a whisky in his room to give Jocelyn enough time to get ready for dinner, he knocked softly on her door.

Louise opened it, curtsied and left them alone.

Sitting at the vanity, in front of the looking glass, Jocelyn positively glowed.

His breath caught in his throat. She looked beautiful. More so than anyone he'd ever seen in his whole life. The gown she wore was the color of lavender, a darker, almost violet colored sash was tied into a huge bow at her back. When she stood, he could see the tails ran down almost to the floor.

He whistled. "Joss, ye look beautiful."

Her cheeks heated. "What did ye call me?" she asked.

"Joss? If ye dinna care for the nickname, I will stop. It fits ye well, though."

She laughed, a light tinkle floating in the air to him. "I like it. I had just grown accustomed to you calling me lass so that it took me by surprise."

"Aye. Ye can be called lass by anyone. 'Tis too generic. Ye needed a nickname unique to ye. 'Twas the first thing that came to mind."

She smiled, bobbing her head up and down, causing the curls in her hair to bounce. "I like it." She offered her hand, and he took it in his, bringing it up to his lips to place a light kiss on her soft skin.

"Ready for dinner?"

She sucked in a deep breath, flattening her palm on her stomach, before breathing it out in a huff. "As ready as I ever will be."

"I think ye will enjoy it. My cook here is on par with Cook at the inn. The two of them could vie for position of best cook in Scotland and I dinna think I would be wrong in stating that it would end in a tie."

Jocelyn's eyes widened. "You've been feeding me so well since I arrived, I fear my hips will grow and grow."

He splayed his hand on her belly. "Ye are eating for yourself and the bairn." He moved his hand to her hips, gently feathering his fingers over the material that hung over them. "And your hips will look amazing with a little more to them." He licked his lips, bent close to whisper to her. "No matter what, ye are the most fetching lass I've e'er seen." Giving her lobe a nibble, he smiled when her breath stilted.

"We best get downstairs, otherwise I'm going to drag ye into my chambers and worship ye as ye deserve."

Her eyes blew wide, her pink tongue peeking out to wet her lips.

"I think I might like that," she confessed quietly.

"Och, Joss. Dinna give me any encouragement." He chuckled and offered her his arm.

Downstairs almost everyone had gathered, and the dining room was alive with conversation and laughter.

Happiness rolled over Gunn as he looked around the room when he pulled out the chair to his right for Jocelyn to sit in. This was what he wanted. Everyone together. It was just that much more special now that he had someone to share his time with as well.

Suddenly, he understood what his friends had been telling him. Once you found that special person, everything clicked into place and the world felt complete.

That's how he felt. Hurdles awaited them, but they'd defeat them together. He was sure of it.

DINNER WAS JUST as delicious as Gunn had promised. He was right when he said his two cooks rivaled each other. They did indeed.

All through dinner, she felt Gunn's eyes on her. Whenever she snuck a look in his direction, he'd catch her gaze. Offer her a wink and a smile.

Her thoughts mulled over the conversation they'd had before dinner. Whilst she dined on roasted duck and braised hare with roasted vegetables, visions of Gunn pulling her through the door to his chamber consumed her. So much so, at one point, she'd needed to fan herself. The room had grown quite heated.

She didn't miss the knowing looks her new friends sent in her direction. Each time they did, she felt her skin flush a little more. She was certain she'd spent the whole dinner red as a beet.

After dinner, the men and women split up. The men went off to do whatever men did whilst the women gathered in the parlor that they'd spoken in earlier, and enjoyed glasses of sherry, and played games of cards.

"I must admit, Jocelyn. Seeing ye and Gunn at dinner, the two of ye make quite the fetching pair," Lizzie stated.

Jocelyn had figured out that Lizzie was surely an instigator. The troublemaker of the group, but all meant in good nature.

"I agree," Clarissa chimed in. "There are most certainly wedding bells in your future," she added.

Jocelyn coughed on the sip of sherry she'd just taken. "Surely, you jest. Have you forgotten I am already wed?"

She pushed her hand through the air in dismissal. "No' for long. Gunn and the rest of the men will make sure of that."

Oh, how Jocelyn wished that time would come sooner rather than later. She looked forward to the days when she no longer had to think of Victor.

Gwen's demeanor grew serious as she gazed at Jocelyn over the cards she held in her hand. "Have ye no' had any word from your husband?"

Jocelyn shook her head. "None at all. Gunn sent Malcolm to Rochester to track him down, but I don't believe he was able to find him, though I think he found out some information from neighbors. I couldn't tell you what though. Neither of them made me privy to the findings."

"'Tis just like them isna it?" Gwen asked. "They go off and do something. Find out some information and then leave ye in the dark. 'Tis frustrating."

Willamina sighed. "'Tis as if they dinna think we can handle the evil in the world. I love that they try to protect us, but we are strong. We willna break with whate'er bad news they're going to tell us."

Jocelyn had to agree. Though she didn't believe for one minute that she was as strong as the rest of the women in the room. They'd all been through so much—and survived. She was in awe of their strength and perseverance.

"Ye are strong, too, Jocelyn," Gwen said, as if reading her mind. "I see your mind going. Not all of our journeys are the same, but they all require strength. Look at ye. Ye made your way from England to Scotland. Alone. And not just the border. Ye are deep into Scotland. That takes strength that I would be hard pressed to conjure up."

She dipped her head. She didn't feel strong. But she supposed she was. She had done something that most women wouldn't even attempt. "You are very kind to say such things."

"She only speaks the truth," Clarissa said. "Before this visit is over, we will have ye convinced of your strength. I promise ye that."

That was how the rest of the evening went. Sipping sherry, playing games. After cards, they moved to charades. Jocelyn laughed so hard, she gave herself a stitch.

Later that evening, when Gunn escorted her upstairs to her room, she found herself not wanting to be alone. She lingered at her door, wanting to be forward enough to tell him what she wanted—him. But not daring for fear of... For fear of what, she thought. Gunn's feelings toward her were obvious. She could tell in the way he carelessly caressed her skin as if it were the most natural thing to do in the world. In the care lighting his eyes whenever he looked at her. In the richness of his voice as he spoke.

So, what was holding her back? A commitment to vows she'd spoken years ago when she was young and naive and believed the world was only filled with good people.

A commitment to someone she didn't love. Hadn't loved in a very long time. Commitment to a man who treated her like property instead of a person. She'd seen Victor treat animals better than he'd treated her.

Damn him. She was not going to let him dictate her life anymore. She was not bound to him. She'd escaped his clutches and was free to do as she pleased. To love as she pleased. Victor would be dealt with, but right now she didn't want to think about him.

She only wanted to think about Gunn. To get lost in his arms and have him kiss all her worries away. To make her feel again.

Live again.

Love again.

"Joss?" Concern creased Gunn's brow. "Is something amiss?"

She worried her lip between her teeth, gathering the courage to do what she longed to do. To say the words she needed to say.

"No. Everything is perfect."

He dipped his head in a small bow. "Then I shall bid ye a good night."

When he turned to go, she reached out, curling her hand around his arm. "Please don't," she whispered, looking at his surprised expression through her lowered lashes.

His eyes dropped to her hand, before he lifted them, and their gazes clashed together. Lifting her hand from his arm to his mouth, he kissed her, letting his lips linger as he stared into the depths of her eyes.

She couldn't look away. It was as if she was entranced. Caught in a spell that she never wanted to be broken.

Gunn didn't speak a word as he gently took her hand and pulled her into his room, closing and latching the door behind them. Pulling her close, so her body was flush against his, he dropped his head and captured her lips in a searing kiss that she felt from the tip of her head to the tips of her toes.

When his tongue sought entry into her mouth, she opened on a gasp, letting him in. Their tongues danced an erotic dance that was wicked and wanton, and she wanted more.

His hands dropped from cupping her face, and his fingers tore at the buttons on his waistcoat, ridding himself of it as quickly as he could, his mouth not leaving hers.

She gasped for air, but she didn't want to break contact.

Walking her back to the bed, he finally broke the kiss, his lips moving to her ear, his tongue tracing the shell, before sucking the lobe into his mouth.

With a groan, she tugged at his cravat, untying the knot so it could fall to the floor. Pushing his shirt off his massive shoulders, he shook himself the rest of the way out of it. Her hands splayed across his pectoral muscles, huge and bulging under her palms. She feathered her fingertips across his skin. She smiled when he shivered, a groan escaping his full lips as he nuzzled her neck, nipping at her skin.

His fingers grabbed the ends of her sash bow and pulled, letting the material pool around her feet. He straightened, looking down at her, trailing his index finger down the column of her throat when she arched her neck back. He dipped the finger into her bodice, finding her nipple and teasing it into a taut peak.

Her breath hitched, and she bit her lip.

Pushing the sleeves off her shoulders, Gunn kissed her skin as he bared it. It pimpled, at first from the coolness in the air, but then from his lips. The feeling was so foreign. Such admiration had never been doled upon her.

She slipped her dress off, letting it fall to land upon her satin sash, and she stood there, in front of Gunn, her shift the only covering she had left. In the past, she'd felt embarrassed in such a situation. But with Gunn? She felt empowered.

Strong.

Sexual.

He toed off his boots and she watched him as he finished undressing. He stood naked in front of her, a feral look in his eyes, as he licked his lips.

Her eyes dropped to his chest, tracked down, following the rippled muscles of his abdomen. She reached out, trailed her fingers along his skin. Smiled when it pimpled under her fingertips. Lower, lower, to the vee of his hips. Down to his manhood. Like the rest of him, it was massive, standing tall. Proud, the tip angry and purple. She touched the tip, and it jerked violently.

Gunn grasped her hand. "I canna have ye doing that, Joss. This night will be o'er much too soon if I do." He smiled wickedly, his eyes flashing.

He released her hand and clutched her shift. His eyes focused on hers, he lifted the gossamer material slowly. It tickled as it drifted over her legs, her hips, her breasts. She lifted her arms, and he pulled it over her head, casting it away.

His eyes blew wide with approval as he looked at her.

"I've said it before, but I will say it for the rest of my life. I've ne'er seen aught more beautiful." His voice was low, gravelly with barely contained passion.

She smiled shyly. Though she didn't know why she suddenly felt shy after being so forward. Deciding to throw her shyness through the window, she wrapped her arms around Gunn's neck, pulling him down to her.

He reached an arm out, drawing down the duvet, and gently eased her back onto the mattress, covering her body with his as he settled between her legs.

"Are ye certain this is what ye want? Ye only have to say nay, and I'll stop. Leave. Find someplace else to sleep tonight."

She shook her head. "I won't allow you to do such a thing. If this wasn't something I wanted, I would not have started it."

He growled, dropping his lips to her neck, nipping at the sensitive skin, causing her to yelp with a giggle.

"I dinna think I've e'er wanted something so bad in my life as I want ye right now."

"I must confess, I feel the same," she whispered, running her fingers through his short hair, scraping her nails across his scalp, making him shudder.

"E'ery touch from ye is heaven, but hot as fire." He kissed his way down the column of her neck, down to her collarbone, then lower until he finally sucked a nipple into his mouth.

She let out her breath on a hiss. His lips were searing. He teased and nipped. Suckled and pinched. Worked her into a frenzy until her nipple was hard as glass. His teeth grazed the taut skin, gently biting, just enough to cause a sting, then he licked away the pain.

As he teased her breasts, he trailed his fingers down her stomach, burying them into her nestle of curls, and found her wet core. His fingers explored. Dipping into her, then retreating, circling the bundle of nerves, that had her thrashing her head from side to side. Her heels dug into the mattress, and just when she thought she couldn't take any more, he shifted his hips and sank himself into her fully. In one long thrust.

She gasped at the fullness, feeling herself stretch around him, to accommodate his entry.

It felt divine.

CHAPTER SIXTEEN

Heaven. Gunn was in heaven. Surely, he'd died and was experiencing the fruits of his labors of life on earth.

Under him, Joss moaned. Deep and guttural. The noise making his cock even harder when he thought it couldn't possibly get any more so.

He wouldn't last long. Already he could feel his bollocks drawing up, tightening, getting ready to release his seed.

Joss's breaths were coming out in short gasps, her nails raking his back. He was certain he'd still have the marks in the morning.

He'd wear them with pride.

Her hands on his jaw, she pulled his face down to hers, capturing his lips in a kiss so deep that he nearly lost his mind.

His hips pumped at a vicious pace, her hands grasped at his buttocks.

He squeezed his eyes shut, clenching his teeth. Trying to hold off until she found release. He pushed his hand between them, finding her pearl, and circled his finger around it.

Her hips lifted, meeting his pace.

Incoherent words spilled from her lips as she swung her head from side to side. Heels planted in the mattress, she brought her hands up to his back once again, her sharp nails piercing his skin as she called out his name.

Her limbs stiffened, and he kenned she'd reached her climax. Her sex tightening around him. Milking him.

Furiously, he pumped his hips, burying himself to the hilt, until he, too, joined her on a mutual climactic journey. He buried his face in her neck as he thrust one last time. Fully buried in her, emptying his seed, as he met his release, his body jerking violently as it overcame him.

It took a few long moments for his body to stop spasming. His breath still ragged, he flipped onto his back, dragging her with him so she could rest her head on his chest.

She turned her face, kissed his chest, before resting her head on him. Her fingers drew lazy circles on his skin, causing him to shudder, as she sighed in satisfaction.

"That was unlike anything I have ever experienced before," she said breathlessly.

He chuckled, lifted his head so he could kiss her hair. "I am glad that I could be the one to give that to ye."

She brought her head up, so she could look him in the eye. "Thank you."

He frowned. "For what?"

"For treating me with such respect. For loving me thoroughly, yet gently. It was," she paused, her blue eyes darkening. "As I said, it was something I've never experienced before."

Laying her head back down on his chest, she sighed in contentment as he stroked her silky hair.

Her husband was a bastard. Jocelyn deserved to be loved like she mattered. Like she was somebody important. And not somebody to be used for whatever selfish reasons her useless husband had. Gunn swore when he saw the bastard he was going to beat the shite out of him so bad that the louse wouldn't recognize himself when he gazed in the looking glass for the rest of his life.

Reaching down, he pulled the duvet over them. It wasn't long before Joss's breathing evened out and he kenned she'd fallen asleep.

He sighed. Her laying in his arms, here, in his chambers, seemed like fate. Like she was born to be here. Wrapping his arms around her, he closed his eyes and fell into his own blissful sleep as if he didn't have a care in the world.

At least for this night, that was true.

IN THE MORNING, when Gunn woke, he found himself alone. He sat up, looking around the room to see where Joss had gone, biting his lip when he realized she more than likely returned to her own room when she'd awakened.

Quickly, he got dressed, then went to the room next door and knocked gently.

He stepped back to wait for her to open the door. After a few long moments, the knob turned, and she opened the door.

"Good morn," she greeted. "I hope I didn't wake you when I left."

He shook his head. "Ye didna. But why did ye leave?"

She poked her head out of the room, looking from side to side down the hall. He assumed to see if anyone was about. There wasn't and she spoke.

"I didn't want to put you in an awkward position. It wouldn't be proper for me to be found in the bed of the laird."

"Joss, honey. Naught of what we did was proper."

She flushed, guilt darkening her features.

He lifted her chin with his finger, drawing her eyes up to him. "That is no' a bad thing. Nor something to regret. I have none." Dark thoughts entered his mind. "Do ye? Do ye regret what happened betwixt us last night?"

He held his breath as he waited for her answer. He wanted her to say nay. Needed her to say nay.

"No," she admitted. Shaking her head. "Not at all."

Relief flooded through him.

"I just didn't want you to lose respect with your staff. Your friends.

I know they mean a lot to you."

"Joss." He pulled her into his arms for a hug. Kissed the top of her head, the scent of lavender in her hair tickling his nose. "My staff ken to mind their business, but they would ne'er say aught or treat ye or me with disrespect. And as for my friends, have ye seen them? Listened to them? They are cheering for our union. Hell, we'll probably go down to break our fast and they'll be able to tell what we've done by looking at us."

She pulled back, a horrified look on her face.

"'Tis no' a bad thing. 'Tis just something that happens. I'm certain we kenned each time they'd done the same. It changes us. Our demeanor." He pulled her closer, close enough that she could feel the effect she had on him, as his hardness prodded her belly. "I really dinna care if they ken. 'Tis what we wanted, aye? Hey." He brought his hands up to caress her cheek. "There's no going back. We're moving full steam ahead. Agreed?"

Worrying her lip, she searched his face. He hoped she could see the truth in his eyes.

Finally, she nodded. "Agreed."

Holding out his hand, he smiled when she accepted it as they made their way downstairs.

⇶✕⇷

WHEN JOCELYN AND Gunn entered the dining room, all eyes turned to them. She couldn't stop the blush that flushed her cheeks. It was as if she'd had what they'd done last night written on her forehead, announcing it to everyone.

The women smiled, and the men smirked.

She sat down quickly. She was so embarrassed she didn't want to look anyone in the eye. Couldn't look anyone in the eye.

If she did, she feared they'd be able to see everything she'd done.

"Ye two are late coming down," Gwen said, pressing her lips together as she tried to hold back her laugh.

Jocelyn threw her hands up and rolled her eyes. "Fine. You all are too intuitive for anything to slip your notice. Jest all you want."

She waited, the quiet lingering for long moments, until everyone broke into laughter at the same time. Loud, raucous laughter.

"We kenned 'twould be just a matter of time," Lizzie confirmed. I mean, we werena going to say aught, but ye told on yourself anyway." She smiled and took a bite of toast that had been slathered with butter and piled high with jam.

Gunn looked around. "Well, now that we've gotten that out of the way." He grasped her hand and squeezed. "Let's enjoy our meal. After we finish, the men and I have an appointment we must attend."

Willamina shot Finlay a narrowed eye look. "Ye didna speak about plans for this afternoon."

He cleared his throat, dabbing the corner of his mouth with a napkin. "'Tis a recent event. We'll be back this eve."

"What shall we do whilst they are away?" Clarissa asked.

"We can walk the grounds. Mayhap stroll the shore," Gwen offered.

"That would be nice," Jocelyn said. She loved the seaside and hadn't had the chance to explore it since she'd arrived.

"I was thinking something more exciting, but we can do that if ye like," Clarissa said.

Willamina scoffed. "Stop making Jocelyn feel bad. I think a walk near the water sounds lovely." Her hands stroked her belly. "I dinna feel up for much else."

"You didn't make me feel bad, Clarissa. Since I haven't seen Leyson Castle before I think I would like to explore the grounds and get to know it. Mayhap we can have afternoon tea near the shore?" Jocelyn suggested, pleased when the other ladies agreed.

Gunn smiled. "'Tis settled then. Perfect." He finished his soft-boiled egg and sipped his tea. Giving her a wink, she tried to come to grips with the feeling that had just overcome her.

Family.

That's what she was feeling. A sense of belonging. She hadn't felt it since she'd left her parents' home when she'd married.

She leaned into Gunn. "Where are you going? Is everything well?"

"'Twill be once we finish. We're going to pay Theodore a visit at his establishment that he funded with my coin."

Her mouth fell open and she raised her brows. "That should be an interesting conversation. His face at your arrival will be priceless."

"I do hope so. I want to see utter shock reflecting back at me."

Worry flashed into her mind. "You'll be careful?" she asked. She didn't know why she worried. Gunn alone was more than capable of holding his own. With the four of his friends accompanying him, Theodore didn't stand a chance. But still, a little niggle of worry ate at her periphery.

"Always. Dinna fash about me. All will be well."

After everyone had finished eating and the serving staff had cleared away the dishes, the men said their goodbyes, promising to return soon.

Jocelyn watched Gunn leave the room, his friends following him out the door.

"Finally!" Clarissa exclaimed dramatically. "I honestly thought they would ne'er leave." She giggled. "I jest. But why should they have all the fun? Let us enjoy the day."

And they did. They froze their toes when they dipped them into the cool sea water and walked along the water's edge. By the time they sat down to nibble on the tea and sandwiches Jocelyn had asked the cook to prepare, their feet were red as tomatoes.

Wrapping hers in the folds of her gown, she squeezed her toes, trying to get the blood flowing through them to warm them up.

"It has been too long since I've spent the day at the shore,"

Willamina said. "'Tis always nice to wallow in the salty air." She sat in a chair near the table that held their luncheon fare.

"I think we need to warm up. 'Tis a beautiful day, but the water was much too cold." Lizzie shivered. "If our husbands were here, they would scold us for putting ourselves into a situation that could make us ill."

"Especially ye, Willamina," Clarissa chimed in. "Finlay would have our hides if ye caught an ague. We would ne'er hear the end of it."

Willamina held up her teacup. "'Tis why I am drinking plenty of tea."

For the rest of the afternoon, conversation flowed easily, as if they'd all been lifelong friends and were doing a weekly meetup. At no point did Jocelyn feel unwelcome. In fact, it was just the opposite. It was as if she was already part of the group and had been from the beginning. The feeling of belonging wrapped around her once again.

After, when the wind began to whip around them as if it were tinged with ice, they retreated inside. Huddling around the gigantic fireplace in the great hall, they stuck out their hands, rubbing them together to warm them.

"I must confess," Jocelyn began. "I can't remember the last time I've had such an enjoyable time spent with friends. Thank you."

"Pfft. No need for thanks," Clarissa guffawed. "We have fun whenever we're together. Wherever we are. Ye'll soon see."

Jocelyn nodded, not knowing what to say. She was just so happy to be there and to be accepted.

"I think I will go upstairs and order a hot bath to warm up and wash the salt off my skin and hair," Gwen announced.

"That's a lovely idea," Lizzie agreed.

"Mayhap after we can all meet in the game room for some bridge?"

They all agreed to a game after they'd bathed, and Gwen and Clarissa checked in on the wee ones.

Alone in her room, Jocelyn wondered how the meeting with Theodore was going. Hoping it went well, she was impatient for Gunn to return.

She'd had a wonderful afternoon with the wives, but she missed Gunn.

Having his arms around her would be the quickest way for her to warm up. She wanted that.

Wanted to feel that every day.

She sighed. Once again her thoughts conflicted. She was falling in love with Gunn. And she was quite certain he felt the same way.

But it was wrong.

Or was it?

CHAPTER SEVENTEEN

"Ye ready for this?" Alexander asked, rubbing his hands together as they approached Theodore's pub. It was housed in a blockade of side-by-side dwellings. White plaster covered the facade. A black iron sign swung creakily in the breeze.

The Toad's Well.

Interesting name, Gunn thought as he pushed open the door and walked inside his friends close on his heels. For a moment, he just stood in the entry, assessing the pub. The space was small. A bar with three stools was straight in front of him, on the opposite wall. Five tables filled the floor space. Dark wooden tables, with matching wooden chairs.

They looked uncomfortable and for some reason, Gunn found that appealing. It was bad enough Theodore funded all of this with Gunn's coin. It would be even worse if it was more comfortable than the Thistle & Pig.

"Gentlemen. Have a seat where ye please. What can I get ye?"

Gunn looked around, but didn't see Theodore in sight. The barkeep wasn't anyone he recognized either. But he had a hunch.

"We'll take your best whisky." The man went to turn away and Gunn called him back. "No' the one on your shelf o'er there." He nodded toward the bar. "The best one ye have. Ye probably house it in the back, I'd say."

The man's eyes lit up and he bowed. "Indeed, sir. Let me fetch your request."

"What are ye doing?" Alexander asked as he watched the man disappear through the door to the back."

"I would lay money down to say that their best whisky is the one that has been disappearing from my own bar."

"Ah." Malcolm sighed. "Good assumption. I'd say ye are more than likely correct."

The door swung open, and Gunn sneered. His hunch had been correct. But even better was a pale-faced Theodore who was bringing out the bottle.

"G-g-gunn," he stuttered. Then he noticed the others. "Your graces. My lords." He bowed nervously.

Alexander pulled out the chair beside him, patting the seat. "Theodore. Come. Sit and have a drink with us."

Theodore shook his head. "Och, I dinna think that's such a good idea. I've work—"

"Sit down," Nicholas boomed. For someone who was normally so quiet, he could be deathly terrifying.

Theodore dropped into the chair, all color drained from his face. He shakily set the bottle of whisky—Gunn's whisky—on the table.

His barkeep exited, and his brows furrowed when he saw Theodore. He puffed his chest out and approached the table. "Is there a problem?"

Gunn stood, a fierce look on his face, and the man's shoulders rounded. "Ye can leave. We've got business with Theodore that doesna concern ye."

"Boss?" He looked at Theodore who looked like he was about to faint.

Clearing his throat, he jutted his chin out. "All is well. I'm closing early."

The man looked suspiciously at the men sitting at the table, his eyes darting from them to Theodore, and back again. Then back to Gunn.

With clenched fists, Gunn took a step forward, and it spurred the barkeep into action. He scooted out the door, flipping the open sign over as he left.

"Now that we're alone," Gunn drawled, sitting down. He picked up the bottle of whisky. 'Tis a fine bottle of whisky. Where'er did ye procure it from I wonder."

"I-I can explain."

"Can ye now?" Gunn leaned on the table, eyes narrowed. "All this time, ye led me to believe that there was something wrong with my business, when it was all your doing."

Theodore put his hands up, shaking his head. "Nay. Nay, that is no' true. Business dried up. No one was coming anymore."

Gunn slammed his fist on the table, causing the bottle to jump, along with Theodore. "Because ye spread word about town that my pub and inn were rat-infested and I was watering down the liquor."

Theodore went to say something, but slammed his mouth shut when he saw the menacing look on Gunn's face.

"How long?" Gunn asked, his voice low.

"Pardon?"

Flanked by Nicholas on one side and Alexander on the other, Theodore looked like a frightened lad.

"How long have ye been stealing from me? Doona e'en try to lie about it. I ken, I just want to ken if ye'll confess to it."

"I, no', er." He gulped air like a fish out of water. "No' long."

Gunn felt his anger rise. "I told ye no' to lie to me." He grabbed him by the lapels of his jacket, hauling him to his feet, so they were nose to nose. "I trusted ye. And as soon as I left, ye started pilfering my coffers."

The man was shaking under Gunn's fists holding him upright. "That is no' true."

Gunn pushed him away with such force that he stumbled back into the table in back of him. He clutched the back of the chair that nearly toppled over for balance and shook his head. "Ye've no proof," he spat.

"Nay?" Gunn questioned. He retrieved the list of transactions that Jocelyn had uncovered and threw the papers at Theodore. "'Tis all right there."

Theodore picked up the papers, his eyes glancing over the amounts, his eyes round in surprise. "Ye ne'er review your books. How?" Then his brows raised as it dawned on him. "'Twas that lassie, wasna it? She put ye up to it. She wanted the money for herself. I warned her to mind her business."

In an instant, Gunn's fist met Theodore's jaw, a disgusting crack rent through the air and the man howled in pain.

"Dinna e'er, and I mean, e'er mention Jocelyn when ye speak. More importantly, dinna try to place the blame on her for your deception."

Gunn backed off, walking around the pub, taking it all in while Theodore whimpered on the floor.

"Here's what's going to happen. Since I have funded most of this establishment, the deed will be signed o'er to me."

Theodore spat blood on the floor. "I willna."

Gunn spun in his direction, approached him. "Nay? Then mayhap I shall go to the authorities and give them the evidence I have uncovered regarding your endeavors. I am certain debtors' prison will do ye some good."

"Ye wouldna," Theodore said in disbelief, his words distorted.

"Nay?" Gunn circled him, as if he were a lion stalking his prey. "Those are your choices. Your only choices." He pulled his watch from his pocket and checked the time. "Ye have sixty seconds to make your decision. The clock is ticking. Will it be option A or B?"

Nicholas pulled him up off the floor and roughly sat him down in the chair at the table.

"All right!" Theodore threw his hands up. "Keep your hands off me. Your grace," he added snidely.

"What is your decision?" Gunn asked.

Theodore's face was swelling, and Gunn was pretty sure he'd broken the man's jaw.

"Well?" He kicked the leg of his chair, causing Theodore to jump.

"What do ye think? I canna go to prison. I will sign it o'er."

"Where's the deed?" Malcolm asked, pushing back from the table. "We'll settle this today."

Theodore glowered at him but mumbled. "It's in the back room. Right side desk drawer."

Malcolm left to go find the paper.

"Once ye've signed it, ye will leave this place at once and ne'er step in it or in the Thistle & Pig again. I dinna want to see ye in town again. I dinna care where ye go, but 'twill no' be here. Understood?"

Nicholas leaned into Theodore, leering at him, and Theodore shrank back, nodding his head. "I got it. Ye willna see hide nor hair of me again."

Gunn smiled, clapping him on the back.

Malcolm returned with the deed, ink and quill. "Sign it o'er," he demanded, pointing to where Theodore needed to sign.

After scrawling his signature across the page, Nicholas and Alexander added theirs to make it official.

"Pleasure doing business with ye," Gunn snapped sarcastically, ignoring the glare Theodore threw his way. "Now, get the fuck out of my pub."

Malcolm and Nicholas hauled Theodore to his feet, dragging him to the door, where they roughly tossed him out on his arse.

Finlay nodded, looking around. "That went smoothly. Nice job." He popped the top off the whisky, and Alexander grabbed glasses from the bar, balancing them as he carried them to the table. "Ye ken, 'tis no' too bad of place. Ye can make it profitable."

"Now that I ken why e'erything was going to shite before and I've eliminated the problem, I've nay doubt."

They all picked up a glass, holding them in the air and clinking them together.

"Slaintè!"

"Ye ken," Gunn said after they each emptied their glass, "that was fun. Reminded me of the old days."

Finlay scoffed. "Ye watch your mouth. Our wives will have our arses if we make this type of thing a habit."

Our wives.

Gunn thought about Joss. It can't happen now for obvious reasons, but he couldn't wait to make her his wife.

AFTER A FUN game of bridge and an early dinner since the men hadn't arrived back home yet, all the ladies decided to go their separate ways and get ready for the evening with their families.

Jocelyn climbed the stairs up to her and Gunn's rooms. They were the only ones on this floor. Louise was waiting for her when she walked into her room.

"I can help ye dress for the night, my lady," she offered, and Jocelyn accepted it.

She enjoyed the help. Appreciated it even. The small talk they would share whilst Louise brushed her hair to a shine was nice.

Once she'd bid her good night and left the room, Jocelyn retrieved her mother's diary from the top drawer of her dresser and sat on the red-cushioned window seat. The huge, bowed window overlooked the garden that led out to the sea. She could see the white caps of the waves crashing onto shore. If she listened closely she could hear them as well.

Opening the diary, she ran her fingers over the pages her mother had written. It was her comfort, this book. A reminder of how life could be.

Should be.

She was getting a glimpse of that now. Seeing what her mother had experienced with her father. The happiness that two people who truly cared and loved each other could experience.

Looking out the window, she wondered when Gunn would return. How things went. If they went as planned or if things went awry and that was why he was late. She hoped all was well.

She couldn't imagine any scenario where the five men didn't come out victorious, but there was always a chance.

Bringing her thumb to her mouth, she nibbled at her cuticles nervously. She didn't want to sleep in here tonight. Alone.

Setting the diary aside, she sat up, an idea forming in her head. But was she daring enough to see it through?

Aye, as Gunn would say, she was.

Cinching the belt of her robe tighter around her waist, she slipped her feet into her slippers and crept over to the door. Pulling it open, she stuck her head out into the hall, looking both ways to see if anyone was about.

The corridor was empty. Not surprising seeing how it was only she and Gunn housed on this floor. And after Louise finished helping her get ready for bed, she would return to the servants' quarters below stairs.

Quietly, she snuck from her room and crept over to Gunn's door. She rested her ear upon it to see if she could hear any noise inside to make her aware that he'd returned. There wasn't any.

Not surprising. She was almost positive that he would have inquired after her upon his return.

Taking a deep breath, she turned the knob and entered the room, closing the door softly behind her. The lanterns had been lit, casting long shadows on the papered blue walls. The fire blazed, adding a warm, cozy feel to the room.

With him not here, she took the time to study his living space. She hadn't been able to see much of it last night. She'd had many more important things to discover. Her body heated at the thought. Strong frissons ran up her arms.

Large, upholstered chairs sat on each side of the fireplace, a table betwixt them. There were books stacked there. She approached and read the titles, but they were not familiar to her.

A painting of what appeared to be the gardens hung on one wall, the sea just visible at the top of the painting. She studied the piece. It was done well. She read the script in the lower corner. Burnett, signed with a big sweeping B.

Had Gunn painted this? He surprised her more and more every day.

At the sideboard, a bottle of whisky and a carafe of wine with glasses were on a tray of silver.

There was a wardrobe, and a dresser on the opposite wall.

The postered bed was flanked by two tables, the intricate designs the same as carved into the bed. A thick blue duvet covered the mattress, with a darker blue blanket folded at the foot. Blue, maroon, and cream pillows decorated the head of the bed.

In front of it, a cushioned bench sat where she pictured Gunn sitting to remove his boots after a long day of work.

She moved to the bed, taking the decorative pillows off and piling them on one of the chairs. Then she slipped off her robe, leaving her only in her thin nightdress, the cool air pimpling her skin. Drawing back the duvet, she slid into bed, settling onto the pillow, and covering herself up.

Suddenly nervous, she wondered if instead of enjoying the surprise, Gunn may be angry with her. Worrying her lip, she ran through different scenarios in her mind.

As more time passed, she wondered if mayhap this was a bad idea. Should she return to her room? But then she thought about Gunn coming to find her this morning after she'd snuck back to her own room.

She got the feeling that he had wanted to wake up with her beside him.

She wanted that, too.

Taking a deep breath, she decided to stay put, and eagerly awaited his return.

Some time had passed, a lot actually, and her eyes were growing heavy. She was wondering if he was going to return tonight, when she heard a knock on the door of her room.

He'd returned!

Her heart skipped a beat, and her pulse quickened.

"Joss?" She heard him call gently.

She could call out. Alert him to where she was, but she wanted to surprise him. She couldn't give herself away, so she waited.

He called out one more time, and when she didn't answer, she heard his footsteps approach.

Holding her breath, she wet her lips as the door swung open.

His eyes clashed with hers the moment Gunn entered the room, flaring wide, a devilish smile on his face.

CHAPTER EIGHTEEN

"Well, arena ye a sight for my tired eyes?" Seeing Joss waiting for him in his bed when he walked into his chambers had his cock roaring to life and fighting to burst out of his trousers. The tension from the day eased from his shoulders, and his disappointment that she'd fallen asleep alone in her own room disappeared.

He loosened his cravat and stalked to the bed, quickly stripping out of the rest of his clothes.

Joss watched him, her lower lip caught between her teeth as her eyes roamed over his body, an appreciative smirk on her face.

"I missed you today."

He slid under the covers and pulled her into his arms, kissing the top of her head, breathing in the cinnamon scent from her favorite soap.

"No' as much as I missed ye. I knocked on your door and when ye didna answer I thought ye had fallen asleep."

She looked up at him, a smile lifting her lips. "I heard you. It took all my control to not go to the door and let you know I was in here. I wanted to surprise you."

Kissing her lips, he smiled against her mouth. "Surprised I am indeed," he murmured.

"Are you mad?"

He frowned as he met her gaze. "Whye'er would I be angry?"

"Because I snuck into your room."

He barked out a laugh. "Joss, ye can sneak into my room e'ery night for the rest of my life, and I will ne'er get angry or tired of it."

She grinned, snuggling into his side. "How did it go with Theodore?"

"Good, I suppose. I am now the proud owner of The Toad's Well pub."

With wide eyes, she laughed. "That's an interesting name." She giggled. "I wonder how he came up with that one?"

"Silly, isna it? I dinna ken. But I think 'tis going to need a rebranding."

"Did Theodore take it well?"

He harrumphed. "No' really. I believe I may have broken his jaw."

She pulled away to look in his eyes. "No!"

He shrugged. "Och, aye. He's lucky I didna do more than that after what he'd done. He e'en tried to serve us my own whisky he'd stolen from my inventory."

"Oh my. That is daring."

He squeezed her close, his hand dropping to run lazy circles along her rib cage. Her nightdress was so thin, it was as if she were naked under the covers.

Which she would be soon.

Her face grew serious. "But he signed the pub over to you. How?"

"'Twas quite easy actually. The sod was flanked by Nicholas and Alexander, and we gave him the choice. Either sign the deed o'er to me since I'd funded the endeavor, or I was going to turn him in to the authorities. He could rot in prison for all I cared."

"Well, he didn't want to do that, obviously." She shivered. "I can't blame him. That would be most horrible."

He dropped his hand lower, caressing her buttocks as she began to squirm beside him.

"Aye, so he signed the deed and then we forced him out, and I told him I didn't want to see him in my town again." He squeezed her cheek, and she squealed.

"Enough about that. I've had ye on my mind all day." He shifted so she was lying beneath him. With a devilish smile, he licked his lips, "And I'm verra hungry."

He scooted lower, pushing up her nightdress as he went, until he buried his nose in the nestle of curls that smelled so sweet.

His tongue darted out, swiping up the seam of her lips, and he chuckled against her as she gasped.

Her hands flew to his hair, not long enough to grasp, but she could still run her fingers through the short strands, her nails trailing over his scalp. Which she did. He was quite sure he'd have nail marks in the morn that would show everyone just exactly what they'd been up to this night.

Sucking the bud of nerves into his mouth, he drew hard on it, as his fingers worked into her moist heat.

Her legs fell open and she ground her hips up.

Smiling, he continued, working her up into a frenzy. Kenning that he had this effect on her was nearly as intoxicating as the act itself.

He felt her body start to stiffen under his hands at the same time she tugged at his shoulders.

"Gunn. I want you. Filling me. I want to feel you."

He growled possessively. "Ye needna tell me twice, love."

Moving up her body, he sank into her wet folds and seated himself fully in her with a shuddering groan.

She gasped, her nails moving to score his back, and he loved every minute of it.

Every scratch would be a reminder, a memory for later.

Her hands moved to his buttocks, adding pressure, spurring him on to move faster.

Much obliged to give her what she wanted, he pumped his hips harder, sweat breaking out on his brow.

Her body went taut, his name spilling from her lips over and over, and with two final thrusts, he moaned loudly. An involuntary shudder shaking him to his core as he emptied himself into her.

If this was how life was to be with Joss, he never wanted to ken another way. In blissful silence he flipped them, reversing their positions.

He caressed her shoulder as their breaths slowed. "Did ye think this was where ye would be when ye walked into my pub all those nights ago?" It seemed like he had kenned Joss forever, but it had only been weeks. Yet in that short time he had come to the conclusion that he wanted to spend the rest of his life with her. By his side. Fathering her children.

The thought of her belly round with a bairn, made him happy. Surely, he would see it soon enough, and it didn't matter to him that the bairn wasn't his. It would be raised as if it were.

She sighed, stretching her arms above her head, her fingers brushing against the headboard. "I didn't. The thought was furthest from my mind. I just wanted to be safe. Far enough away from Victor where he would never find me."

Placing a kiss on her forehead, he let his lips linger there. "He will ne'er hurt ye again. I can promise ye that. As long as there is breath in my body, his hands will ne'er touch your skin again. In any way."

She turned to him, lifting on her elbows. "How did I e'er get so lucky to find a man as kind as ye?"

"I think I am the lucky one." He tucked her head under his chin. "Let's sleep. 'Tis been a long day."

She murmured something but he couldn't make out her words and soon she had fallen asleep, her breaths slow and even as they fanned the hairs on his arm, tickling them.

For the longest time, he just lay there, listening to her soft snore. Reveling at the feel of her body against his, as if they were made for each other.

This was how he wanted to spend every night.

As the days passed, Jocelyn enjoyed her time getting to really know all of Gunn's friends. He treated the women like sisters, and the men were truly his brothers.

But as much fun as the days were, she most looked forward to the nights. That was when she and Gunn would retire to his chamber and get lost in each other's bodies.

By this point, she was certain she knew every nook and cranny of him. What each scar came from. The places where he was more sensitive to touch than others.

And most importantly, the things that made him growl like a wild animal, unable to control himself any longer.

She found she really enjoyed an out of control Gunn. Her face heated just thinking about it.

Gwen, always the intuitive one, noticed right away. "What has ye blushing this time, Jocelyn?" She giggled, already knowing the answer. They all did.

And instead of being embarrassed like she would have been before, Jocelyn joined in on the bawdy laughter.

They were outside, enjoying the day by playing a game of badminton. Playing in two teams of a pair each, Willamina sat nearby, keeping score, her hands taking turns between massaging her back and her very large belly.

"If I didna ken any better, Willa, I'd bet ye are having twins," Gwen stated.

"Och, dinna say such things. The doctor said there is only one bairn growing."

Gwen shrugged and Clarissa chimed in. "Doctors can be wrong. If ye dinna have two bairns in there, that one bairn is going to be birthed a tot."

Willamina waved her hand in dismissal. "Enough talk about my incessantly huge belly. Let's talk about something, or someone else." She winked and focused her attention on Jocelyn.

"When should we plan on attending the wedding?"

Jocelyn flushed. "You know that can't happen right now. Not until, well, you know. Until Victor is dealt with."

"Hmm," Lizzie said. "I must say I am surprised that between all the men, they've been unable to locate the louse. He must be hiding well."

"But why would he hide?" Clarissa asked. "He surely, by law at least, has e'ery right to lay his claim and insist upon Jocelyn's return."

She hated how they spoke as if she were property, but she also knew it was true. In the eyes of the law, she was Victor's property. Just as if she were a prized pig in the city square.

It was funny how she always felt that way with him, but when she was with Gunn, or any of his friends, watching how they treated their wives, with love and devotion.

As equals.

The feeling was completely different.

"Mayhap he will stay in hiding and ye willna have to deal with him e'er again."

She sighed. The thought was tempting. "If he does, then Gunn and I will ne'er be able to marry. At some point, he must show his face. Either in Rochester or God forbid, here."

"Malcolm has some associates watching around Rochester. If your husband shows up there, he'll ken."

If she and Gunn could get away with living the rest of their lives as they were today, with no repercussions on either side, she would gladly do so. But she also didn't want to be Jocelyn Townsend anymore. The name left a sour taste in her mouth.

She very much looked forward to being Jocelyn Burnett as soon as possible.

Gwen served the shuttlecock and Lizzie swung and missed, giving

Gwen and Clarissa the point.

"Ha! That's the game," Clarissa hooted, punching her fist in the air.

Lizzie rolled her eyes. "We won the first one," she announced, pointing her finger between herself and Jocelyn. "We need to play a tiebreaker."

"I'm ready to keep score." Willamina waved her hand in the air. "Winners get to serve first."

"Ha!" Clarissa stuck out her tongue playfully and lobbed the shuttlecock to Gwen to serve.

The serve was fast, but Jocelyn hit it back.

Clarissa swung and hit the shuttlecock in such a way that it didn't arc, just a straightforward hit.

Jocelyn lunged for it, her toe catching in a rut, and went tumbling forward, her ankle twisting painfully. She landed in an unladylike thud and the others gathered around her, faces pinched in concern.

She grabbed her ankle, putting pressure on it to stop the immediate throb of pain.

"Oh my God, Jocelyn," Gwen exclaimed, dropping beside her on her knees. "Let me see," she said in a motherly voice and Jocelyn got the impression she'd had to use that voice more than once, whether it was with her siblings, Nicholas's siblings, or her own children.

With a grunt, Jocelyn lifted her foot.

Tenderly, Gwen prodded at her ankle, apologizing when Jocelyn hissed in pain. "Sorry. The good news is 'tis no' broken. But ye've definitely sprained it." She set her foot on the ground gently. "Clarissa, can ye run inside and get some yards of linen? We should wrap it to prevent it from swelling further." She turned back to Jocelyn. "Ye'll need to stay off your foot for a while. Mayhap e'en a month."

Jocelyn cursed her clumsiness.

"'Tis no' your fault," Lizzie offered. "'Tis Clarissa's. Did ye see the way she hit that thing?" She smiled widely, letting her know she only jested. "But dinna blame yourself. "It could have been any one of us. Well, except for Willa, who is happily sitting there watching."

"I would gladly trade places, Lizzie," she said dryly.

"Nay. I dinna need twins. I dinna e'en need one, which I would think would be enough at a time."

"For the last time. I am no' having twins."

Clarissa returned with strips of linen and Gwen wound them tightly around Jocelyn's ankle, taking care to not cause any more pain as she worked.

Lizzie and Clarissa offered their shoulders, stooping down to allow Jocelyn to put her arms around them. Slowly, they helped her stay balanced as she hopped on one leg back to the house.

Later that night, when Gunn carried her upstairs to their room, because that's what it had become—theirs, he set her gently on the bed and helped her undress and slip into her nightdress.

"'Tis going to be sore for a while. Ye twisted it good."

She looked down at her foot, at her swollen, purple toes. "I should have been more careful," she scolded herself for the umpteenth time that day.

"Och. Were ye having fun?"

Laughing, she nodded. "I was until this happened." She pointed to her foot and shook her head. "Just what I need. For you to carry me around all day long."

"Whilst I would enjoy that, ye're light as a feather, on the morrow we'll find some walking canes to assist ye some. But dinna attempt the stairs on your own," he warned, his voice low and stern. "Ye'll fall and break your pretty neck."

He moved to the other side of the bed, pulling the duvet down. Then fluffed her pillows before lifting her easily and laying her gently on the bed. He grabbed two more pillows from a cupboard and stacked them under her injured ankle.

"Ye should keep it elevated to help with the swelling."

"You are much too kind to me. Have I ever told you that?"

"Plenty." He bent, capturing her mouth in a searing kiss.

Wrapping her arms around him, she tried to draw him closer.

"Nay, lass. No' tonight. I dinna want ye to injure yourself further." He climbed in beside her, turning on his side, resting his head on his hand. "And ye've nay idea how much that pains me."

CHAPTER NINETEEN

It had been a week since Jocelyn had injured her ankle. She could finally put light pressure on it and was able to get around on her own for the most part. Gunn was glad. She was beginning to resemble a caged animal, ready to burst through her confinement at the slightest chance.

"Ye certain ye'll be fine with me away?" he asked for the hundredth time that morning. He and his friends were going to spend some time letting off steam with whisky and boxing.

"I'll be fine. I believe the girls and I are going to get lost in a competitive game of bridge." She smiled, trying to placate him of his guilt for leaving her.

"If ye need aught..."

"I won't. Go. Have fun. Just go easy on the others," she teased.

He captured her mouth in a kiss. Savoring her taste. "I want more of that later," he stated, and left her in the drawing room, her laughter following him out the door.

The five men made their way into the town, deciding to get away from Leyson for the day. To see and talk with some of their friends that they hadn't conversed with in some time.

"Drinks first, then boxing," Alexander announced.

"Aye," Nicholas said dryly. "That way we can all be pissed when Gunn punches us to oblivion."

He chuckled, "I would ne'er."

"Dinna deny it. We've seen ye this week. Lots of," Malcolm

paused for dramatic effect, "frustration ye need to work out. Might as well be in the ring."

They were all laughing as they entered one of the gentleman clubs they'd frequented often. Choosing a table in the corner, they took their seats. Gunn signaled for a server. "Five glasses, and a bottle of whisky, please."

The young lass curtsied and hurried off to fulfill their order.

He scanned the room. It was quite busy, a lot of the tables filled. He waved to a few familiar faces. An unfamiliar couple of men sat at one of the tables, heads together as they discussed whatever it was they talked about. Probably business, by their clipped tones.

Three single men sat at the bar. He didn't recognize any of them, and they stuck to themselves. Quietly drinking, ignoring everyone else in the pub.

Their drinks arrived and they cheered their thank yous as the server set their glasses on the table with a clank and then poured them each a serving of whisky, leaving the half empty bottle on the table when she left.

Holding up their glasses, they all called out *slaintè*, and took a long pull of whisky.

The men at the bar turned to them to see what all the ruckus was about but quickly turned back to their own glasses.

"Willamina looks like she is going to have the bairn any day now, Finlay. Any hour, actually," Alexander said.

Finlay sighed. "Aye. I've made peace with the knowledge that she will give birth here, rather than at home."

"Ye ken ye are welcome to stay at Leyson as long as ye need."

"Thanks, brother," Finlay said, lifting his glass and emptying it in one long pull.

Every once in a while, Gunn felt like he was being watched, but whenever he looked up and scanned the crowd, no one was paying attention to him. He chalked it up to the whisky and pushed it to the back of his mind.

After they'd finished their second bottle of whisky, they stood, and Gunn approached the bar; two of the three men sitting there previously remained. He settled the bill, and they left, making their way to the fighting club.

They secured one of the rings, and as they wrapped their hands and knuckles to prepare, jested each other incessantly.

The next three hours were spent taking turns with one another in the ring, whilst the others cheered them on from the side.

"Hey, watch the face," Alexander called, dodging a right hook that Nicholas swung. "'Tis been years. Ye canna still be mad that I married your sister. She's well cared for." He jabbed at Nicholas, catching him in the shoulder.

Nicholas swung, caught him on the chin. Alexander grunted and hopped back. "Your sister willna be happy if I arrive home bruised."

"Ye talk too much. Mayhap Gunn can break your jaw, like he did Theodore, and save us all from your incessant yammering."

"That was uncalled for," Alexander grumbled.

The two of them kept at it for another quarter of an hour before they jumped out of the ring, exhausted, breathing heavily, but otherwise unscathed.

This has been a fun day. We needed this," Finlay announced. "'Tis been too long. We need to make it more of a habit."

"Agreed, 'tis been hard with all that has happened," Malcolm said. "Mayhap if ye stop getting your wives with bairns 'twould be easier."

"Or," Alexander drawled, "ye and Lizzie can start a family and join in the shenanigans of fatherhood."

Malcolm sighed. "We're trying. Lizzie is keeping a strong face, but she's upset that she hasna conceived yet."

Nicholas clapped him on the shoulder. "Give it time. 'Twill happen when the timing is right."

Malcolm nodded, but Gunn could see the flash of pain that flickered across his face.

"Well, gentlemen. This has been fun, but I think we should make our way back home to our better halves," Gunn said. What he really wanted to say was their wives, but of course, Jocelyn wasn't his wife yet.

Yet.

She would be.

Hopefully soon.

WHEN THE LADIES called for tea, Jocelyn excused herself. She was tired and wanted to lie down for a bit.

"Are ye sure?" Lizzie asked, concern furrowing her brows.

"Yes, I fear I haven't been sleeping much at night and it has caught up with me. I will take a nap and be back down."

She hopped away as the women guffawed behind her.

It seemed to take her forever to get to the house. She could put some weight on her foot, but not her full weight so she needed to make her way slowly over the uneven landscape to the castle.

Inside the door, she leaned on the frame, catching her breath. A movement behind her caught her attention and she turned to see her worst nightmare.

Victor stood there, a sneer slashing his face, his dark eyes almost black as he advanced.

"Y-y-you are not welcome here."

"Well, lucky for you I am not here for a visit, Jocelyn. I am here to collect my wayward wife."

Her eyes darted around the space. He was blocking the door that led outside. She wouldn't be able to push past him if she tried. Her injured foot would be a deterrent.

Spinning, she moved toward a door that she hadn't seen used since she'd arrived. Mayhap it would lead her outside.

Ignoring the pain in her ankle, she ran to the door and pulled it open, but as she tried to tug it closed behind her, Victor was there, pulling it open. Leaving it, she moved into the small platform and the stairs that disappeared into the inky darkness below. She had no choice.

As she clung to the wooden railing to assist her down the stairs, she felt Victor's hands on her back, pushing her forward.

She held onto the railing for dear life. If she let go, she'd go tumbling down and injure herself even more.

"Stop pushing me," she cried. Finally, she reached the bottom, but the space was only an empty stone room. Her breath was coming in short spurts. Victor would kill her down here.

There was another door, and he swung it open, shoving her inside.

Grabbing her shoulders, he pushed her hard against the stone wall, and she knocked her head against it.

The space was dark, and she couldn't see, but she could feel the anger roiling off of Victor in violent waves.

"You left me. Do you know how long it took me to finally track you down?" he asked, spittle spraying her face.

A tear slipped down her cheek. She really thought she had run far enough that he would never find her.

She should have known better.

"Do you?" he shouted when she didn't answer.

The sting of his hand slapping her cheek made her cry out.

Grasping a handful of her hair, he pulled her down to the ground roughly. "You shouldn't have run," he ground out in her ear.

She tried to remove his fist from her hair, but he wouldn't relent. Her scalp stung from the pull.

"You thought you could leave me?" he snapped close to her face; she could feel his breath on her skin. The next slap should have been expected, but it still took Jocelyn by surprise and she cried out.

"Shut up!" he screamed as he took his anger out on her and she could do nothing but put her arms up in defense.

Noise from upstairs stopped Victor's assault and he covered her mouth with his hand.

"Do not say a word or I will slice your throat right now." To emphasize his statement, he pressed something to her neck.

She froze as the cold metal met her skin.

She had no doubt that he would fulfill his promise.

Silent tears flowed down her cheeks. What had she done?

⇶⇷

THE MEN LEFT the fighting club and called for their carriage to take them home to Leyson. It was one of Gunn's larger carriages, but with the size of the men, they were forced to squeeze together. But it was better than arriving separately and missing out on all the conversation.

At Leyson, they piled out of the carriage and loudly made their way inside.

Outside, the women were in the garden having tea.

Except Joss. She was nowhere to be seen.

"Where's Jocelyn?" he asked, the hairs on the back of his neck standing up.

"Inside," Lizzie said. "I believe she's resting. We didna want to wake her."

His brows furrowed. "How long has it been since ye've seen her?"

The women looked at each other, shrugging, murmuring.

"A half hour," Gwen said. "Mayhap an hour at the verra most."

Gunn rushed into the house. He didn't ken what it was, couldn't put his finger on it, but something didn't feel right.

They all followed him inside. He took the stairs two at a time, running down the hall to his room.

Empty.

He pushed open Joss's door. But he kenned it would be empty as well. She never spent any time in this room anymore.

"She's not here," he called out.

They spread out, half inside, half outside, methodically making their way through the house, floor by floor. Outside they checked the gardens, the shore, the outbuildings.

Meeting back in the house, his friends all shook their heads.

She had to be here somewhere. She wouldn't leave. Gunn's heart beat so hard, he could feel it pounding against the walls of his chest.

"The storage rooms."

"What?" Malcolm asked.

"Downstairs, the root cellar. The storage rooms. 'Tis the only place we havena checked. We ne'er go down there." He spun on his heel, rushed to the door that would lead him down the narrow steps to the earthy atmosphere below. Pausing, he grabbed a lantern and lit the stairs, and he breathed a sigh of relief.

She wasn't at the bottom lying in a crumpled heap.

He whispered a prayer of relief, but he noticed the disturbed dust. The marking of footprints on the steps. It had been a long time since anyone had been down here. They didn't use these rooms anymore, so the staff stayed away.

Turning to the others, he held his finger up to his lips, hushing them.

He listened intently. And there it was. Whimpering.

Jocelyn!

How the hell had she gotten down here?

"Joss!" he called out. "We're coming! Are ye all right?"

She didn't answer, which made him fash even more. Mayhap she had fallen and knocked her head. She shouldn't be on her feet, never mind going up and down stairs. Now wasn't the time, but he would make sure she kenned better once he got her back upstairs.

Downstairs, he held up a lantern and followed the scuff marks to the closed door that led into the root cellar portion of the space.

Why would she close herself in there? Something wasn't right. She wouldn't do this on her own.

He turned. "Ladies, go upstairs," he ordered, his voice low, lethal.

"We want to—" Clarissa started, but Malcolm, realizing the severity of the situation silenced her with a look.

"Go. We will be up shortly. With Jocelyn," he added, when she refused to move.

With one last look trying to see over his shoulder, she straightened and nodded.

As the women disappeared upstairs, the men came together, speaking in hushed tones.

"What do ye think has happened?" Nicholas asked, looking toward the door.

"Joss wouldna have come down here out of curiosity. Something, or *someone*, chased her here."

"Townsend?" Malcolm whispered.

"'Tis my guess. I'm going to kill him."

His friends looked to each other, nodding. "Here we go again. We've got your back, brother."

Hand on the knob, Gunn twisted and pushed, the uncoiled hinges squeaking loudly in the small space, echoing off the cold, stone walls. As soon as the door began to open, Joss screamed.

"Look out!" Jocelyn screamed.

A man rushed forward, knife in hand, catching Gunn in the shoulder. The slice burned, but he ignored it with a grunt, swinging out his arm and catching the man in the throat. He collapsed on the ground, trying to catch his breath.

But he wasn't done. He kicked out his leg, catching Gunn in the back of the knee.

Keeping his balance, he moved into the room, and he heard his friends drag the man away from the door. They'd secure him until he could ensure Joss was okay.

He found her crouched in the corner, loud, racking sobs escaping her mouth. When she looked up, he saw her battered face, the beading of blood on her neck.

That fucking bastard! Wanting to go out and pound the fucker's face into pulp, he needed to be strong for Joss.

Dropping to his knees beside her, he assessed her wounds, trying to keep his anger in check, but failing.

"'Tis okay, love. I've got ye."

She leaped into his arms, wrapping herself around him, and sobbed into his neck, her whole body shaking. "I, I. He walked into the house. I d-don't know how. I ran, slow, because of my ankle. He blocked the d-door. I thought, m-maybe d-down here would lead outside."

"Shhh," he coaxed, stroking her hair, trying to get her to catch her breath.

"You are laying with my wife!" Townsend spat from the other room. "I'll have you hanged. Oof!" Gunn couldn't see, but he kenned the sound of a punch to the gut well.

Jocelyn winced, her breath coming normally now. She pulled back to look at him. "I thought he was going to kill me. But then we heard you, and he stopped. She lifted her hand, and her eyes widened, her gaze moving to his shoulder. "You're bleeding."

He tore off a strip of his shirt and dabbed at her nose. "Ye are, too." He shrugged off her concern. "Dinna fash. We need to get ye upstairs. E'eryone is fashed."

Picking her up, he settled her into his arms. "Ye all right?"

She nodded, and he exited the room, took note of Townsend doubled over in the corner and carried her upstairs. The women surrounded them as soon as he walked up the stairs.

"Och!"

"Jocelyn!"

"Lay her on the sofa. We will see to her," Gwen said, shooing him away. She grabbed his arm and looked at him fiercely. "Ye do what ye need to do. She needs to be free from that monster."

He nodded, then hurried back downstairs.

His friends had Townsend in a chair. The man looked at him with a sneer.

Quite daring for a man in his position. And also one that looked like he had to beat on women because he sure as hell couldn't beat on a man.

"You're fucking my wife," he spat. "*My* wife."

"Real men dinna treat their wives with heavy hands and beatings."

"She needs to be reminded of her place."

Gunn's fist met with the man's nose, a vicious crack sounding, and Gunn kenned he'd broken it.

He grasped his face, trying to staunch the blood. "You bastard. You broke my nose!"

"Aye. How's it feel? How do ye like being on the other side of a fist?"

He swung again, catching him in the ribs. And again, to the ribs, knowing they were cracking under the weight of his fists.

Malcolm pulled him off. "Enough, brother."

"Ye have nay right to her anymore. Got it? Ye will divorce her, set her free, and ne'er step foot in Scotland again, or I swear to God, I will be sure ye ne'er take another breath."

"Are ye threatening me?" Townsend wheezed, his ribs making it hard to breathe.

"Ye tried to kill a laird. That will no' go o'er well for ye," Finlay said. "In the presence of two dukes, no less."

"And two earls," Nicholas added.

"Now, I will secure ye a ride back to Rochester. My solicitor will draw up the papers. They will be to ye tomorrow. I suggest ye sign them."

"We'll accompany him to ensure he does," Malcolm and Alexander said in unison.

Gunn nodded, leaving them to get Townsend gone.

He needed to check on Joss to ensure she was okay.

>>><<<

HER CHEEK HURT and she had a hard time seeing out of her right eye when she awoke the next morning. On the bright side, it took her mind off her ankle.

Turning to the side, she caught Gunn beside her, watching her intently. "How do ye fare this morn?"

She smiled, the movement causing her scabbed lip to break, making her wince.

"I know I must look a sight," she said slowly. "But my heart is happy."

He smiled, the gesture transforming his face which had been set much too seriously.

Grasping her hand, he brought it to his lips. "I was so fashed. I dinna ken what I would have done if I had lost ye."

She pushed herself into a sitting position, her hands coming up to his cheeks, her thumbs stroking his jawline. "But I'm here. All is well, yes?"

"Ye will have your divorce, aye."

Her heart jumped as happiness filled her. It was as if a huge weight had been lifted off her shoulders. "We can marry?"

"Aye," he said happily. "We can. As soon as ye feel up to it."

She frowned, remembering she wasn't the only one who had been wounded. "Your shoulder. How is it?"

He blew off her concern. "'Twas naught, really. Just a small cut."

There was so much blood. She knew he was downplaying the injury.

"Rest now. I'll have some food brought up for when ye wake.

Then we've got a future to plan." He gave her a lopsided smile.

"I canna wait," she said in her best Scottish brogue.

His brows lifted in surprise, and then he bellowed with laughter. "Ye can talk to me like that all day long, love."

"I'll be right back." He got off the bed and headed to the door.

"Gunn?" She called.

"Aye?"

"I love you."

"I love ye, too, Joss. More than ye can e'er ken."

EPILOGUE

Eight months later

"Let me see my wee lass," Gunn purred as he lifted Winnie from Jocelyn's arms. "The older she gets, the more she looks like ye." He kissed the bairn's silky hair, her big blue eyes looking at him.

He was so proud of Joss. She'd birthed their bairn like a warrior. And Winnie was their bairn. Their daughter. Two months ago, Winnie entered the world, crying so loud he was certain the world could hear.

He and Joss had been inseparable since that horrible night. They'd married as soon as Gunn had received the signed divorced papers. Malcolm and Alexander had seen to that. He was quite sure there may have been some prodding by fists to make it happen but happen it did.

"Where's my niece," Gwen called from the other room, carrying her newest bairn, Freddie, and burst through the door. "They're in here," she called over her shoulder. Nicholas, carrying Violet, followed, with Bennie clinging to his trouser leg, his thumb stuck in his mouth.

Gwen stopped short. "She's a beautiful wee lass, isna she, Nicholas?"

"Aye," he said, clapping Gunn on the shoulder.

Clarissa and Alexander entered next, Colin on Alexander's shoulders, holding on to his ears for balance. He pointed to his son. "And this is why my ears are always red," he laughed. "Lovely to see ye three. Congratulations on the arrival of your wee one."

"Thank you," Joss said quietly, and Gunn kenned she was getting overwhelmed with emotion. He squeezed her shoulder. "Ye all right?"

She nodded, grabbing his hand.

"Did someone say we needed more bairns in the house?" Finlay called before entering the room, carrying his son, Allan.

Willamina followed him, carrying their daughter, Anna, Allan's twin sister. As they'd learned, the doctors weren't always right.

Last to arrive were Lizzie and Malcolm. She pushed her way through the door, her round belly leading the way. It wouldn't be long, and their family of two would become three.

Gunn looked around the room. At his brothers. Their wives. Their bairns and wee ones, and smiled, pride filling his chest as his and Joss's gazes met.

They'd all come so far. From boyhood friends, to brothers-in-arms, to husbands, and fathers.

And it was because of all these strong women. Without them, none of this would be possible.

He bent to Joss, placing a kiss on her cheek.

"I love ye, Joss."

She smiled, pulling him in to capture his mouth before whispering, "I love you, too."

About the Author

Award-winning author Brenna Ash is addicted to coffee, chocolate, and all things Scotland and BTS. She's a firm believer that one can never have too much purple or glitter. She loves rom-coms and always cries at the HEAs.

When she's not busy writing about sexy, Scottish Highlanders, Medieval Pirates, Regency Rogues, or co-hosting the true crime podcast, Crime Feast, she spends her time reading with her favorite music playing in the background, binge-watching Outlander and Bridgerton, park-hopping with her besties, spoiling her cat, Lilly, or watching BTS content online. Brenna lives with her husband on the Space Coast in sunny Florida.

Website – www.brennaash.com
Amazon – amazon.com/stores/author/B01H46ZA02
Facebook – facebook.com/BrennaAshAuthor
Instagram – instagram.com/brennaashauthor
BookBub – bookbub.com/profile/brenna-ash

Printed in Dunstable, United Kingdom